Emily Harvale lives
– although she wo
French Alps ... or Ca
has several months ᴏɪ ꜱɴᴏᴡ. ᴇᴍɪʟy ʟᴏᴠᴇꜱ
snow almost as much as she loves Christmas.
Having worked in the City (London) for
several years, Emily returned to her home
town of Hastings where she spends her days
writing ... and wondering if it will ever snow.
You can contact her via her website, Twitter,
Facebook or Instagram.
There is also a Facebook group where fans
can chat with Emily about her books, her
writing day and life in general. Details can be
found on Emily's website.

Author contacts:
www.emilyharvale.com
www.twitter.com/emilyharvale
www.facebook.com/emilyharvalewriter
www.instagram.com/emilyharvale

...

Scan the code above to see all Emily's books on
Amazon

Also by this author

The Golf Widows' Club
Sailing Solo
Carole Singer's Christmas
Christmas Wishes
A Slippery Slope
The Perfect Christmas Plan
Be Mine
It Takes Two
Bells and Bows on Mistletoe Row

Lizzie Marshall series:
Highland Fling – book 1
Lizzie Marshall's Wedding – book 2

The Goldebury Bay series:
Ninety Days of Summer – book 1
Ninety Steps to Summerhill – book 2
Ninety Days to Christmas – book 3

The Hideaway Down series:
A Christmas Hideaway – book 1
Catch A Falling Star – book 2
Walking on Sunshine – book 3
Dancing in the Rain – book 4

Hall's Cross series
Deck the Halls – book 1
The Starlight Ball – book 2

Michaelmas Bay series
Christmas Secrets in Snowflake Cove – book 1
Blame it on the Moonlight – book 2

ISBN 978-1-909917-70-5

Published by Crescent Gate Publishing

Print edition published worldwide 2021
E-edition published worldwide 2021

Editor Christina Harkness

Cover design by JR and Emily Harvale

Emily Harvale

Dreams and Schemes
at
The Seahorse Inn

CRESCENT GATE PUBLISHING

This dedication is from one of the lovely members of my Readers' Club and is in her own words, to someone very special to her.

To Kevin, loved and missed forever.
Diana x

Map of Seahorse Harbour

There's an interactive map, with more details,
on my website: www.emilyharvale.com

One

'I really want this one, Portia.'

Portia Trulove dragged her gaze from her rear-view mirror. She had been captivated by the vivid crimson hues of the sunrise and the bright yellow sun piercing its way through the remnants of the storm clouds behind her. Now she smiled at her dad's face on her hands-free mobile.

'I know you do, Dad. And don't worry. I'll get it for you. Have I ever let you down?'

Tommy Trulove chuckled.

'Not once, sweetheart. Not since the day you were born. I know I can count on you. But Seahorse Harbour's different from the others. The local council is far more rigid and the planning rules and regs are stricter there than anywhere else we've built.'

'Then I'll just have to be even more charming and persuasive, won't I? Don't worry. It'll work out fine. There'll be a Trulove luxury hotel in Seahorse Harbour by this time next year.'

She was nothing if not optimistic. They didn't yet own Seahorse Harbour Holiday Park, the site on which they planned to build the latest addition to their prestigious hotel empire, but that fact didn't faze Portia at all. Thanks to the Trulove's contacts, she was certain the site was as good as theirs.

She was sure theirs would be the first offer. It was also a very generous one for such a relatively small site, so even if the vendors hesitated to agree, the estate agents would no doubt advise them that it would be the best price they were likely to get.

Once the Truloves owned it, they would need to demolish the current buildings, fell several trees in a portion of the woodland called Little Wood which was included in the sale, remove all the static mobile homes, excavate the entire site, including the pool area which would be enlarged and rebuilt as a far superior infinity pool, have all main services redirected, and build a luxury hotel.

Okay, a year was pushing it, but if anyone could do it, Portia could.

'I have complete confidence in you, sweetheart. Are you there yet?'

'Almost. I'm just driving up to the top of Seahorse Cliffs.' She surveyed the surrounding scenery and gasped as she sped to the top of the hill and saw the expanse of cliffs and the tiny village itself, laid out before her. She braked hard and stopped to admire the view. Other than her red Audi TT, there were no cars on the road. In fact, she hadn't seen another vehicle since she'd left the Easterhill Hotel and Spa, which was where she had spent the previous night. 'Wow, Dad! You weren't exaggerating when you said this place is beautiful. It's absolutely breathtaking. I can almost see the hotel now.'

She remembered every inch of the digital plans of the architect's drawings and in an instant, had positioned them in her mind's eye, on the site of Seahorse Harbour Holiday Park, visible in the distance.

The holiday park occupied a small but prime site to the west of the little village and from her extensive research Portia knew it was open year round, apart from two weeks at the end of January and the first few days of February.

It was the first of April today and coming into the Easter weekend, so in theory the place should be buzzing with holidaymakers, but it wasn't quite 7 a.m., so most people were probably still fast asleep in their beds. She couldn't see any sign of movement, although from where she sat, the holidaymakers and residents alike would look like those matchstick people in a Lowry painting.

Portia was an early riser and was always up before the sun and out with the larks, as her dad often said. She had never actually seen a lark, or heard one for that matter, but she liked the expression. A lark sounded like a happy bird, and that's how Portia greeted each new day. With a smile and an optimistic outlook.

She was definitely optimistic today. She couldn't wait to reach her destination and see Seahorse Harbour Holiday Park in all its glory, but her appointment wasn't until 9 so she'd have a rather long wait.

Plenty of time to explore the village and perhaps meet a few of the residents. Assuming some of them were up and out this early. But Thursday was a work day so surely someone would be?

She'd read that the holiday park consisted mainly of static mobile homes that could be rented for anything from a weekend up to an entire season, but there was also an area where people could bring their own caravans, or even tents, and rent the space for the same time periods. Although most caravaners and campers probably only stayed for a week or two.

She could see the colourful static mobile homes and could definitely make out some caravans and a few tents but the place didn't look exactly heaving. Which was probably why it was up for sale. Well that, and because of the age of the current owners. Retirement no doubt beckoned.

'Seahorse Harbour Holiday Park first opened in 1930,' her dad had told her, and her own research had confirmed that. 'It was called Seahorse Harbour Holiday Camp in those days and most of the accommodation was in tents, but there were three brick-built chalets with running water, electric light and modern toilets, which were considered luxurious. The rest of the site shared a small toilet and washroom block, but again, with water, lighting and toilets, it was regarded as plush.'

'Really?' Portia had laughed at that.

Running water, electric light, and modern toilets were considered basics now, together with heating, a Wi-Fi connection, and a large screen TV with satellite channels. Even in a place like Seahorse Harbour Holiday Park. At least they were if the resort wanted to compete with its rivals.

Any standard hotel room had all those things, together with a telephone, safe, mini-bar and a hairdryer.

A standard, Trulove Hotel Room, known as a Classic Room, also had air-conditioning, free Wi-Fi, a trouser press and a bathrobe and slippers. But it also had a jacuzzi bath, a walk-in, waterfall shower, voice-controlled and activated lights, blinds and curtains, along with similar controls for the heating, air-conditioning, showers, TVs and all the other gadgets.

A Trulove Deluxe Room had all that, plus a balcony with a private plunge pool and a view of the sea or mountains, or of a site of special interest, if situated in a city.

The ultimate in luxury – a Trulove Regal Suite, was twice the size of a Deluxe Room, and the private pool was larger and usually an infinity pool. The suite came with its own butler, plus everything any guest could want. Literally. If a guest requested something, no matter how bizarre, the hotel would endeavour to get it for them – assuming it was legal, and also morally and ethically okay to do so. The Truloves, and especially Portia, drew the line at certain things. They wouldn't arrange for guests to hunt and kill animals, for example.

When Portia had been in training, in her late teenage years, at a Trulove Hotel in Scotland, without even consulting with her dad, she had banned grouse shooting shortly before the start of the season. The fact that it was one of the major draws for many guests, which led to several cancellations and complaints, didn't worry her at all. It was something she felt strongly about, which was what she told her dad. She also informed him she wanted to ban all shooting and hunting of living birds and creatures at every Trulove Hotel. Luckily, and perhaps unsurprisingly, as Portia always got her way, when she called her dad and told him what she'd done, he backed her decision, in spite of the fact that it cost them a few extremely wealthy clients.

'We believe in preservation of all wildlife,' Tommy Trulove hastily announced to the press, 'and all our hotels will now follow the Trulove code of ethics.'

They quickly put together that code and it won them new, and in many cases, equally wealthy clients who believed in saving not just wildlife, but the planet as a whole. It also garnered them a great deal of free publicity.

Seahorse Harbour Holiday Park had no such luxuries or extras to offer its clients. But back in 1930, it did have a few, in addition to the water, light and flushing loos. There was a brick-built, carpeted sun lounge with easy chairs, which offered spectacular views of the bay. This alone was one of the biggest selling points at the time, but it also advertised itself as having a Lido, which in reality was little more than a paddling pool, judging from old photos Portia had seen. Now that Lido rivalled the Olympic-sized pool at Easterhill Hotel and Spa, and sun loungers sat on a pristine, white-tiled area, with tables and chairs placed on a raised concrete section behind. At one end of the pool was a row of outdoor showers and at the other end, a row of water jets where children and adults alike ran back and forth as the jets shot up around them. At least that's what the photos on the website portrayed.

In the early days, there was a dining hall and a fish and chip shop on the site, plus a small but well-stocked bar, both of which were definitely an added draw. Now there was a small ice cream parlour called Ice Dreams, a pizzeria called Pool Pizzas, with bistro-style tables and chairs outside, a hotdog kiosk, and a much larger bar. But none of these held a candle to what was on offer at a Trulove Hotel.

The site did own a section of a woodland though, oddly called Little Wood even though it wasn't that little, but the rest of the woodland was common land. Little Wood ran from just across the road from the beach and up behind several of the cottages in the village and on for a couple of miles. It also stretched for almost a mile and a half behind the holiday park itself.

Portia had read that during the Second World War, the holiday park had been occupied by the RAF, and the dinky village, which from where Portia now sat in her car, looked more like a model village than a real place where people actually lived, had become a strategic point in Britain's defences.

Many holiday camps around the country were requisitioned by the British Government to avoid the need to spend time and money building purpose-built camps. Some were used for training or for stationing troops. Others as internment camps, or for housing refugees. Some for other necessary workers. Several camps were so badly damaged during this period, not only from bombing raids and such like but also from the troops and other occupants themselves, that they had to be rebuilt or razed to the ground.

Seahorse Harbour Holiday Camp fared better than most, and over later years the owners made improvements and changed the name from Camp to Park but like other such places, it suffered when the boom for holidays abroad took hold. Now the current owners were retiring and the place was up for sale.

The Truloves intended to knock it all down and replace it with one of their hotels, once they got their planning permission approved. And once they owned the place, of course. But that was a foregone conclusion as far as Portia was concerned and she was here today to seal the deal.

Not that a deal had actually been done.

The site had only just come up for sale, but thanks to their contacts, she was certain she and her dad were the first ones to be aware of that fact. They'd get in before anyone else had a chance. That's how they always acquired the sites they wanted. Why should Seahorse Harbour Holiday Park be any different?

'I knew you'd love it,' Tommy said, now. 'I know I did the first time I saw it. I think it might become one of our best hotels.'

Portia wasn't sure about that. The site was too small to make the hotel exceptional.

The drawings were certainly spectacular though. Her dad had said that no cost was too high for this hotel, which was a surprise in itself. The compact size of the site meant the hotel would be one of the smallest in the Trulove portfolio, so for her dad to say that costs didn't matter, was most unlike him.

But Portia already knew that this project was more than just a property transaction to him. This one was personal too. He hadn't actually told her that, and he'd poo-pooed the notion when she'd mentioned it, but she knew her dad better than anyone, and Seahorse Harbour, and this proposal, definitely meant something special to him.

She was equally surprised when he said he wanted her to run point on it. It wasn't the first time he'd handed over complete control to her, but it was the first time that he hadn't wanted to visit the site for himself. Even just once.

'I don't need to see it, so I won't be going with you,' he'd said when she'd told him she was booking their rooms at the Easterhill Hotel and Spa and arranging a date for the trip to the site and wanted to check that was all okay with him. 'I can recall what it was like. And besides, that's what the internet is for. I can see the satellite map view whenever I want.'

'But you always go on the first visit, Dad.' She couldn't hide her surprise. 'And you've said yourself, those maps aren't always up to date.'

'Believe me, sweetheart, those maps could be ten years old and they'd still be up to date where Seahorse Harbour is concerned. Nothing ever changes in that village.'

She grinned mischievously. 'Everything's going to be changing in the village once we get approval.'

Tommy laughed. 'That's very true. And I can't wait to see her ... their faces, when we do.'

'*Her*, Dad?' Portia had picked up on his quick change of words. 'Is there something you're not telling me? Something I should know about Seahorse Harbour? Or its

11

residents?' She'd kept her tone light, but her stomach was twitching in an odd manner.

'What? Goodness, no, sweetheart. Just a slip of the tongue, that's all.'

But Portia wasn't convinced. Was there a woman in the village who meant something to her dad?

She laughed at her suspicions. A woman who meant something to her dad? That was a joke. The only woman who had ever meant anything to Tommy Trulove was her own, long-dead mother, and the only women who meant anything to him since his beloved first wife's death, were Portia herself, and Portia's younger sister, Bethany.

Tommy's five other wives were merely passing fancies. And all were fleeting. They'd also all had pre-nups before he married them, and on each of his five other weddings he'd taken Portia – and as she got older, Bethany, aside and told them the pair of them were the only women who meant a nugget to him. And that they were the only women who would ever get their hands on his hotel empire.

'Let's see how long this one lasts?' Portia had said at his third wedding. She'd reckoned about a year, which was one year less than his second marriage – and she was spot-on. The others hadn't lasted much longer, either.

'Right, Dad. I'm going to say goodbye and go in search of breakfast.'

'Didn't you have breakfast at the hotel?'

'Nope. Just coffee. I thought it would give me a chance to chat to some of the locals and see what the jungle drums are saying. You know there's always gossip in a village like this. No one should know we're interested yet, unless the vendors have told them, but it'd be good to find out what the locals hope will happen with the site.'

'You're always one step ahead, sweetheart. Enjoy your breakfast. Let me know how things go. Drive safe.'

'Always. I'll call you later. Bye.'

With one final look at the vista before her, she put her foot on the accelerator pedal and roared towards the village.

Two

'What, exactly, are you saying, Diana?'

Dazed by the words he'd just heard, Mikkel Meloy raked his free hand through his windswept blond hair, which seriously needed a trim, screwed up his eyes and held the phone as close to his ear as possible.

He wasn't sure he'd heard her correctly. How could she, after all these months and everything that had happened, be calling him so early in the morning and telling him she desperately needed to see him? To be with him.

He tried to block out the thunderous roar of the waves crashing against the cliffs only a few metres from where he stood and the ha-ha-ha-ha of the gulls circling overhead. The damn things literally seemed to be laughing at him.

Frown lines crinkled along his forehead and his brows knit together as he listened to Diana's fractured breathing, as if it might give him some clue as to what was going on in her head. Some clarity. But the silence now was deafening.

'Diana? Are you still there?'

'I'm here.'

Her reply was soft. And somehow, infuriatingly sexy.

How crazy was this?

Just hearing her voice still turned him on.

He wasn't entirely convinced his heart had healed from the last time she broke it, but he was sure he couldn't risk it happening again.

'I ... I can't go through it all again, Diana. Not unless, this time, you're sure.' He swallowed the massive lump of anxiety that had formed in his throat and gave a small cough to clear it. '*Are* you sure?'

She'd told him things weren't working out between her and Alex; that recently she awoke in the middle of the night and wished she hadn't taken her husband back. That she believed she may have made a mistake.

Mikkel's fingers tightened around the phone as he waited for her response.

'I don't know, Mikkel.' Now her voice sounded tearful and pleading, as if she hoped he had the answers to her dilemma and could solve it for her. 'I'm so confused. I'm not sure of anything at the moment. But I am sure of one thing. I miss you. I miss us. I ... I love you.'

His heart wanted to soar with the gulls and to laugh back at them.

But she had said this before. Twice, in fact.

And then she'd dumped him and gone running back to her husband.

Why should this time be any different?

'And what about Alex? Do you still love him?'

'Y-yes.'

He could hardly hear her. 'Yes?'

Her sigh was soft and sorrowful. 'I know that's not what you want to hear – and I wish I could say I didn't. But I do. I think I always will. He's the only man, other than you, that I've ever slept with. The only man I've loved. Until you. And he's the father of my children. You must understand, Mikkel. There'll always be that bond between us.'

Mikkel hardened his voice. And tried to harden his heart.

'I do understand that. Of course I do. What I don't understand is why you're calling me at 7 in the morning and telling me you need to see me. Why are you saying you love me and you need me in your life, if you still love Alex?'

'Because I do, Mikkel! I ... I love you both. I can't bear the thought of losing you.

Permanently losing you, I mean. I ... I know you'll think this is stupid, but I had a dream about you last night. It was so real, so vivid, so ... frightening. I had to call you and tell you how I felt. How I feel. I had to let you know I *do* love you and ... and that there might be a chance for us. If ... if I can make myself see sense. You're such a good man, Mikkel. You're loving and loyal and trustworthy. Alex said his cheating days are over and I wanted to believe him. You know that.'

'Yes. That's why you dumped me and went back to him, isn't it? So what's changed?'

'I don't know! Sorry. I didn't mean to snap at you. But I don't. I'm being honest.'

'Has he done it again? Has he slept with someone else?'

'No! At least, not to my knowledge. And he's been here every day since ... the incident at Christmas, so he hasn't really had a chance. He's trying so hard. And things have been better. They truly have. But ... I discovered something a few weeks ago. At Lottie and Asher's engagement party actually. And it's ... it's made me feel differently, somehow. I can't explain it and it doesn't really make sense, but I'm not sure Alex will ever change. I do believe he wants to, and I also believe he's trying his best. But ... well ... I think he may simply be addicted to sex. And not just sex, but having affairs. I think there's something in him that makes him incapable of being faithful, no matter how much he might want to be.'

Mikkel was tempted to say, 'I think I could've told you that.' Instead, he said, 'I'm sorry, Diana. I know how much you wanted it to work.'

'Thank you, Mikkel. You're so understanding. I knew you would be. I knew I could count on you. Can we meet today? At your house, perhaps? I can get away after breakfast. I'll tell Alex I'm meeting Josie and we're going shopping for the day. We can spend the whole day together, Mikkel.'

He sucked in a breath as the gulls laughed louder, or so it seemed.

She wasn't coming back to him. At least not yet. She just wanted a meet-up and she was going to lie to her husband about it. Did she want to talk? To discuss whether she would leave Alex once and for all and start a life with him. Or did she just want a day of illicit sex?

He missed having sex with her as much as she'd told him she missed having it with him. But he wanted more than sex. He wanted a relationship. A commitment. Love. A future together.

'Diana, I ... I'm not sure that's such a good idea.'

He heard the tiny gasp of surprise.

'What? Why not? Don't you want to see me? Don't you ... don't you care about me anymore?'

He let out a sigh and shook his head. 'I want to see you more than you can imagine – and yes, of course I care about you. I ... I think I still love you, God help me. But that's the problem, Diana. I can't spend the day with you, and build my hopes up, just to have them smashed to pieces again. That's not fair to me – or to you. Or to Becca and Toby. Your kids need stability in their lives. And, although I can't believe I'm saying this, it's not fair to Alex either. I ... I think, perhaps, you need to work this out for yourself. You need to decide which one of us you want to spend the rest of your life with. Seriously. I don't want to simply have another affair with you, Diana. If anything is going to happen between us again, this time it has to be for real. You have to choose, once and for all.'

'But ... I need to see you, Mikkel. We need to talk. I ... I miss you. I miss being in your arms. I miss your kisses. I miss making love with you. Just one day, Mikkel. Please! Just today. And then I'll decide. I promise. Oh God. I've got to go. Becca and Alex are coming into the kitchen. I'll call you back.'

'Diana? Diana?'

Mikkel cursed loudly as the screensaver

image of his hometown in Norway replaced the caller ID photo of Diana's beautiful face and stunning smile.

The bloody woman had rung off.

He raised his arm to throw his phone, but sanity prevailed and he laughed mirthlessly with the gulls at his stupidity and swore several times to release his frustration.

He spotted the gleaming red bonnet of the Audi TT, racing towards him, about two seconds before he heard the squeal of brakes, as loudly as the mocking laughter of those bloody seagulls.

Three

'Holy crap!' Portia tumbled from her car and stared dumbfounded at the man lying face down on the grassy bank at the edge of the road. Not far off, the waves were pounding the cliffs below and swooshing against the sand and shingle so loudly that for just one second it sounded as if the cliffs might crumble into the sea. She ignored them as best she could, shook off her bewilderment and yelled across to him. 'Are you okay?'

He was clearly alive because, not only was he moving and possibly trying to get to his feet, but he was cursing loudly. He was well-built, tanned and fit, she couldn't help but notice, and he had a striking profile, although his tousled blond hair could do with a trim.

'I'm lying on the grass verge, having been mown down by a maniac, and you ask me if I'm okay! Do I look okay?' His voice was strong and gravelly with an edge of anger and frustration.

'*I'm* the maniac?' Portia didn't bother to hide her sarcasm; the man was clearly fine. 'Excuse me, but I wasn't the one standing in the middle of the road. And I didn't even touch you, so you can hardly say I "mowed you down", can you?'

'It's a good thing I saw you racing towards me and managed to dive out of harm's way.'

'I braked hard the second I spotted you. We're both lucky there are no other cars on this road. Were you trying to get yourself killed? Do you have a death wish or something?'

She stuck out her chin and tossed her golden blond ponytail over her shoulder.

He had managed to sit up and he swiped at the clumps of mud splattered all over his clothes, as he finally turned his head to face her and glowered at her with intense, blue eyes, which at this precise moment were filled with a mixture of exasperation rapidly giving way to astonishment.

'I was merely crossing the road. We don't expect people to treat these roads like racetracks.'

They glared at one another and she scrutinised every inch of him in a matter of seconds, the sound of the sea fading into the distance as she gave him her full attention.

Flipping heck. The guy was gorgeous. He seemed to be having difficulty in standing up and she mellowed instantly as she hurried to his side.

'You're okay though, aren't you?'

He blinked several times and when he spoke again, his tone had also totally changed, as had his demeanour. He even gave her a small and somewhat nervous smile. And that made him even more attractive.

'I'll live.' His smile broadened.

'I'm relieved to hear that.'

Now they were gazing at one another like embarrassed, tongue-tied teenagers, but she couldn't look away as she returned his smile. Those incredible, blue eyes. The dark blond, now raised, brows and firm, stubble-covered jaw. The princely-shaped nose. The tanned, smooth-looking skin. That full, currently half-open mouth that was just asking to be kissed. Wow!

After a few moments he gave a small cough and once more attempted to get to his feet but he stumbled as he stood up and Portia pulled herself together and stepped even closer to help him.

She caught him in her arms and the bolt of electricity that surged through her took her completely by surprise. Their eyes met for a second. Had he felt it too?

He quickly looked away and it was just as well he managed to steady himself because there was no way Portia could've stopped him from falling. The man was solid, streamlined muscle and much taller than he'd looked sprawled across the grass.

'Thanks,' he said, pushing a thick lock of wayward hair from his face as she stepped away from him.

'Anytime.'

He brushed several blades of grass and a few petals of spring flowers from his faded blue jeans and fisherman-style, pale grey jumper and as she watched his agile hands, a strange tingling sensation ran up and down her arms.

She was tempted to help, but thought better of it. Just looking at him seemed to be having a very odd effect on her.

Perhaps it was delayed shock. She had almost run him down, after all, even though she wasn't going to admit that to him.

She glanced back at her car and closed her eyes for a moment as the realisation of what might have happened, dawned on her.

The skid marks didn't lie. Her car now sat at a slight angle to the road and the boot was directly opposite where the man had landed on the grass verge. He was right. If she hadn't braked so hard and he hadn't dived out of the way in time, they would be waiting for an ambulance right now.

Her hands started shaking. She couldn't stop them.

'Are you okay?' the man asked, glancing down at her with genuine concern in those amazing eyes.

He was a good eight inches taller than her and she craned her neck slightly to meet his look as she shoved her hands into the pockets of her black leather jacket and managed another smile.

'Yes. Are you?'

His brows met and he gave her a curious look and another gorgeous smile.

'Yes thanks. But are you sure you're okay? You look as if you're shaking.'

'Shaking? No. Um. Perhaps I'm cold. It's still a bit chilly, isn't it? But it's early and the sun's only just up. Did you see the storm last night? I thought it was the end of the world or something. The windows of my hotel room actually rattled.'

What was she going on about? She cleared her throat and smiled harder.

'Your hotel room? Are you staying nearby?'

'Easterhill Hotel and Spa. Do you know it?'

'Yes. It's a very nice hotel. You should've been in my bedroom. It – Oh! I didn't mean that quite the way it sounded. What I meant was that the storm sounded worse in my bedroom. I live right by the sea. On the edge of the cliffs, a little farther down this hill. I could hear the waves crashing against them for most of the night.'

'You live here? In Seahorse Harbour?'

He nodded. 'Yes. You can see my house from here.'

He half-turned and pointed to a massive house just a few metres or so down the road. It seemed to be perched near the cliff edge but had clearly stood there for many years. It looked very old, maybe Georgian, or even earlier. It was difficult to tell because most of it was screened from view by trees and bushes.

'Wow. That looks impressive. Have you lived there long?'

'Not long. I only moved to the village a couple of years ago.'

'With your wife?'

His blond brows furrowed.

'I'm not married.'

'Me neither.'

She cleared her throat again. This wasn't like her at all. Anyone would think she was the one who had been knocked down the way she was behaving.

'Good to know. Are you staying at the hotel with ... someone special? Or friends or family?'

'None of those. I'm on my own.'

'Business or pleasure?'

'Both, I hope.'

'Ah. You should never mix business with pleasure.'

He smiled and winked and her heart did a little flip.

'Business is a pleasure, to me, so I always mix them.'

'What business are you in?'

Damn. She didn't want anyone in the village to know that yet.

'Er. Tourism. And you?'

'Me? I own a pub in the village. It's the only pub in the village, to be precise. The Seahorse Inn. And a restaurant. Hippocampus. Plus a nightclub which is next door to that, called Neptune's. And a holiday rental called The Boathouse.'

She raised her brows and grinned. 'It sounds as if you own half the village. It's not very big, is it?'

'The village? No, it's not.'

'I assume the pub was already here, and possibly the restaurant, but is the nightclub a new-build, or did you buy that as is, or redevelop other buildings?'

He cocked his head a fraction and seemed surprised by her question.

'The pub's been here for centuries. The restaurant and nightclub are both new-builds, on what was once an old boatyard. Which is where The Boathouse is situated. That's original and has been there for more than one hundred years. But it's not what you might think. It's actually an old sailing lugger turned upside down, with the bow cut off and boarded up, part of which forms the door.'

'That sounds intriguing.'

'It's certainly a tourist attraction but it's bijou, to say the least. A man called Harry Boatman lived there his entire life until he died at the age of one hundred. I've kept it as true to its origins as I could but when I bought it, all it had was a chair and table, a pot-bellied stove with its chimney pushed through the hull of the boat, a few shelves and a bed made from the remaining wood of the bow. I've had to update it a bit, and I managed to squeeze in a shower and a toilet.'

'I'd like to see that.'

'I'll be happy to show you around. Are you staying long?'

'A few days or so.'

'And where were you off to in such a hurry? Are you visiting someone in the village? Or were you just speeding through?' He grinned at her and brushed another lump of mud from his right knee.

'Oh. Er. I haven't had breakfast. I was hoping there would be somewhere open in the village.'

He raised his brows. 'Didn't you like the choice of breakfast on offer at the hotel? I thought it was fairly extensive. Certainly better than anything you might get in Seahorse Harbour. No. That's not true. You'll find the best breakfast you've ever tasted, down on Sea Walk. Which is just as well because it's the only place open at this time in the morning. It's the Seahorse Bites Café, which I can highly recommend. The menu isn't vast but the food is delicious and the owner and her nephew are lovely people. Sea Walk is the promenade. You can usually park in Sand Lane but as it's almost the Easter weekend, there may not be any spaces, so feel free to park in the pub car park instead. It's just a few seconds away from there.'

'*Your* pub car park? That's very kind. And thanks for the recommendation. I didn't eat at the hotel because service doesn't start till 7 and I'm an early riser and wanted to be out and about before then. Breakfast starts at 6 at our ... at the hotels where my family and I often stay.' She'd almost let the cat out of the bag. 'Have you had breakfast? Perhaps I could buy you some. As a sort of apology. Not that I'm admitting anything, you understand. You were standing in the middle of the road, after all.'

He grinned at her. 'Let's say we're both equally at fault. And no. I haven't had breakfast. I was on my way home to do just that when...' The grin melted away and his voice trailed off.

'When you were almost hit by a car.' She laughed nervously.

'What? Oh. Er. Yes. Um. Breakfast sounds good. Thanks. But I think I should go home and change.' He smiled down at himself and his mud-splattered clothes.

'I can wait. Why don't I drive you to your place and wait while you get changed? That way you can show me where your pub is, and the café.'

He shot a look at her car as if he had some doubts but a second later, he smiled.

'That sounds like a good plan. I'm Mikkel, by the way.' He held out his hand. 'Mikkel Meloy.'

She took his hand in hers but there was no bolt of electricity this time. There was something though. An odd sort of feeling: like their hands were two pieces of a jigsaw puzzle that slotted together perfectly.

'Hi Mikkel. I'm Portia.' She hesitated for a moment. He might not have heard of the Truloves, but then again, he might. Probably best not to give her surname for now. 'Mikkel doesn't sound English. And, I may be wrong, but do I detect a slight foreign accent? Nordic, perhaps?'

He nodded approvingly. 'I'm originally

from Norway. A town called Hell, which is approximately thirty kilometres northeast of Trondheim.'

'I know Hell! My dad, my sister Bethany and I have been there. It was several years ago but I've got the obligatory photos of the three of us standing beside the sign at the railway station, and the one on the Hell Bru Bridge over the river. We've been lucky enough to visit many places in Norway, but of course, seeing the Northern Lights, and also polar bears in Svalbard were the highlights. We've recently ... er ... talked about returning.'

She'd almost done it again! She'd nearly blurted out that they had recently opened a Trulove Hotel much farther north and closer to Alta, but she'd stopped herself in the nick of time.

She, Bethany and their dad had travelled across a good deal of Norway over the years. Her dad loved the place.

Her fourth step-mum had been Norwegian. Tommy had met Inger on a trip they took to see the Aurora Borealis, or the Northern Lights as they are more commonly known, for Portia's twenty-first birthday. Inger was there from Oslo.

That marriage only lasted three years, but Tommy's love of the country remained steadfast and he was determined to have a hotel in Norway at some stage.

The site for the Trulove Aurora Borealis Resort Hotel, had once been a campsite. It was just a few kilometres from Alta, on the banks of a small fjord with an area of unspoilt spruce forest, and was another of Portia's successful acquisitions.

'Wow,' Mikkel said. 'They say it's a small world. I was probably living in Hell when you were there.' He smiled as if that thought not only pleased but amazed him. 'My dad still lives there, but he comes to visit me often.'

Portia's tummy grumbled loudly and she hid her embarrassment with laughter.

'I think I need that breakfast. Are you okay to walk or do you need some help?'

'I think I can manage.' He took a few steps and smiled. 'Yep. I'm good. But you will promise not to try to run anyone else over between here and the village, won't you?'

'Cross my heart.' She made the sign of a cross and walked towards her car. 'But you're going to get changed first, aren't you?'

'I think I've dried out now. And besides, I'm not sure you should wait.'

'That's a shame. I was rather hoping to get a peek at your house.'

'You're welcome to come and take a look around at any time you like.' He stopped beside the passenger door and glanced over the roof at her. 'Do you have plans for dinner tonight?'

She beamed at him. 'I think I do now.'

He beamed back. 'Yes? That's great. I'll pick you up at 7 from your hotel. We can have cocktails at my house and you can have a look around, followed at 8 by dinner at Hippocampus. The food is superb, even if I say so myself.'

'I don't doubt it.' She leant both forearms on the roof. 'I've got a better idea. Let's meet at 8 at your restaurant and then go back to your house for a nightcap and a tour. That way, we can take our time and we won't have to rush because there's a table waiting.'

He held her gaze and his smile turned almost devilish.

'That's definitely a better idea.'

She matched his smile.

'Uh-huh. And if there's another storm, I might even get a chance to hear what it sounds like in your bedroom. Just for a moment or two, of course.'

His mouth fell open and she giggled to herself as she got into the car.

Four

Mikkel took every chance he could get to dart a surreptitious look at Portia as he gave her directions to the car park of The Seahorse Inn. She could've used her sat-nav but what was the point? The car park was only a few minutes from where her car had been straddling the road.

As they drove down Seahorse Cliff road towards the centre of the village, he racked his brains for something clever to say, having failed to think of a witty response to her comment about being in his bedroom.

Unfortunately, he couldn't get that thought out of his head and visions of this stunning woman being in his bedroom late at night while a storm raged outside were making him feel uncomfortable. Both mentally and physically. He shifted in his seat more than once during the short drive but he hoped she hadn't noticed.

Thankfully, she did appear to be keeping

her eyes on the road and her attention focussed on her driving. She was also staying within the speed limit of 30 miles an hour, which was both a relief and a surprise.

There was something about Portia that made him certain she liked to live life to the full and a risk or two wouldn't bother her.

What gave him that impression, he wasn't sure, but he suspected spending time with her would be frustrating and exciting in equal measure.

Again, images of her in his bedroom pervaded his thoughts and he almost jumped out of his skin when his mobile rang.

He pulled it from the back pocket of his jeans, glanced at the screen and Diana's beautiful face, and a pang of guilt shot through him.

But what did he have to feel guilty about? His affair with Diana was over months ago. And he wasn't the one who ended it.

He wasn't the one who wanted to start it up again, either. Although less than half an hour ago, when Diana had asked to come round, he had been sorely tempted to say yes. It was only his determination not to have his heart broken all over again that had made him say she needed to make a decision, once and for all.

'Don't mind me,' Portia said, darting a

smile at him. 'I can pull over if you want to take that and need some privacy.'

He shot a look at her, swiped the red 'decline call' icon and shoved the phone back in his pocket.

'No. It can wait.'

She giggled softly and it sounded both delightful and sexy at the same time.

'I hope that wasn't your girlfriend.'

He laughed in response. In a more manly fashion, he hoped.

'No. Just a friend. I don't have a girlfriend. I wouldn't have asked you to dinner if I had.' A sudden thought niggled him. 'Er. Do you have a boyfriend? I know you said you're not married, and I can see you're not wearing an engagement ring, but is there someone special in your life?'

She raised her perfectly arched brows and grinned.

'Apart from my dad and my sister, no. No significant other. I don't really have much time for relationships. I can't even recall my last date. Oh wait. Yes, I can.' She laughed and shook her head. 'The less said about that one the better.'

'Not a match made in heaven then?'

'More a blind date from hell. Oh. Not from your Hell. A blind date from there would be heaven if all the men look like you.'

Their eyes met and heat rose between

them. Or perhaps he was the only one feeling that. But her cheeks looked flushed even through her tan.

'Thanks,' he said.

She coughed quickly and continued, 'He was from the biblical hell and he brought his own fire and brimstone. He actually lectured me on the way I was dressed. Can you believe that? And when I asked for a glass of wine, he looked as if I'd asked for poison or something. Needless to say, I didn't stay to drink it. I'd have been wishing it were poison if I had spent another second with him. A well-meaning friend set us up, but she hadn't met him either. He was the brother of someone she knew from her mother and toddler group. Sorry. I'm waffling. What was your last date like? Better than mine, I suspect.'

'Um. Not brilliant.' The last date he'd been on was with Diana. 'Turn left here. This is my pub. Drive past and turn left again into the car park.'

She darted a look to her right and then bent her head and looked left at the pub as they drove past.

'That church opposite is beautiful. I must take a better look at that later. And so is your pub. It looks just as I knew it would. Ancient, quaint and cosy.'

'The opposite of me, I hope.' He laughed

and smiled at her.

'Oh I don't know,' she teased, parking the car merely inches from one of the bushes bordering the car park.

'The church is called St Mary Star of the Sea and there's some debate about which came first. The ancient oak tree in front of it or the church. But the church was built around 1069, so it was probably that. The bench is a much later addition, obviously.' He laughed again as they got out of the car. 'It's a great place to sit on a warm evening. You can look straight down either Lower Church Hill or Sand Lane, to the sea and the expanse of sky, which is filled with stars on a clear night.'

'You're a romantic?'

'Does that surprise you?'

She tilted her head to one side.

'No. What's the story there?' She nodded towards the gardens across the road from the car park and the frontage of the pub.

'That's Memorial Gardens. A splendid hotel stood there once, but it was bombed in the Second World War. I've got some photos hanging on the walls in the pub of what it was like in its heyday. The steps you can see lead down to lawned areas and bushes and plants and a path meanders through them to the promenade. The perfume from those plants is glorious in the summer when the pub windows are wide open.'

'It couldn't have been a very large hotel. Your pub, the church and those cottages over there all look as if they've been here forever.'

They walked towards the promenade.

'Not quite forever, but yes, they predate the hotel. I'm not really the best person to ask about the village as I've only been here for a couple of years, but some of the locals will be able to tell you anything you might want to know. And probably a lot you don't want to know. I think the hotel was built in the mid-1800s. It was three storeys high and ran the full length of the road down to the promenade. I believe it really came into its own when visitors came to take the waters once those bathing machines became all the rage. But don't take that as gospel.'

'It's a shame there's no longer a hotel here, don't you think?'

He hesitated for a split second.

'There's the Seahorse Harbour Holiday Park. That's over there.' He nodded to his right in the direction of the holiday park. 'But you have to like sleeping in static mobile homes, caravans, or tents, to stay there.'

She grinned. 'Not really my style. I like comfort and a few luxuries.'

'There's a pool. And you'll get the best hotdogs you've ever tasted. Or pizza, if you prefer. And the ice cream sundaes are a treat on a hot, sunny day.'

'Tempting, but no thanks. I prefer a hotel.'

'Well, you never know. Maybe there'll be one in Seahorse Harbour before too long.'

'How do you know that?'

She sounded surprised and also a little cross as she stopped in her tracks and stared at him.

'What's wrong? I thought you said you prefer hotels.'

'I do. I ... I'm just surprised, that's all. Are you saying there's talk of a hotel being built here?'

He glanced from side to side. 'I shouldn't have said anything, but yes. Seahorse Harbour Holiday Park is up for sale and it's the perfect setting for a small hotel. Please keep this between us, but I'm seriously interested in acquiring the site and building an eco hotel. I've already had a meeting with the owners and we're in negotiations. I'm fairly confident of getting it.'

He beamed triumphantly. He hadn't meant to tell her but he couldn't help himself.

Except she didn't look as impressed as he'd hoped she would.

'Portia? Are you unwell? You look as if you've seen a ghost.'

Five

Portia tossed her handbag onto the passenger seat, crunched the gears into first and sped from the car park as fast as she could.

This couldn't possibly be happening.

For the first time in months, she'd met a man she found attractive. A man who made her feel things she hadn't felt in years.

She'd enjoyed flirting with him, once she'd realised she hadn't killed him, and that he was also interested in her.

When he'd asked her to dinner, she was sure she was going to end the night in his bed. Or he'd end up in hers at the hotel. She'd been looking forward to getting to know him better over breakfast.

And then he'd dropped that bombshell.

At first she'd assumed the owners of Seahorse Harbour Holiday Park had let the cat out of the bag about her scheduled meeting with them this morning. But then it became clear that Mikkel had no idea anyone else was interested in the site. He clearly knew nothing of her 9 a.m. meeting.

He was her competition but he didn't know it.

And he wanted to build an eco hotel!

Dear God. An eco hotel? Was he one of those 'save the planet' type of guys?

She had nothing against them, of course, and on most levels, she too wanted to save the planet. But not at the expense of comfort. Which is what a hotel should offer. Not composting toilets, rainwater showers, and lighting and heating run by solar or wind power.

His concept for the site couldn't be more different to hers.

But the fact that the owners hadn't informed him another party was interested, told her all she needed to know. This would come down to money.

Mikkel owned a pub, a restaurant, a nightclub and a holiday rental. He also owned a rather grand looking home. But unless he was hiding his wealth, he would be no competition for the Truloves. Tommy Trulove was on The Sunday Times Rich List. She was fairly certain Mikkel Meloy wasn't.

When he'd said she didn't look well, she had seized her chance to get away and think.

'Actually, I don't feel that great, all of a

sudden,' she'd said. 'I think, perhaps, I'd better not risk breakfast and I'd better go and lie down.'

'We can go to my pub,' he'd said, taking her by the arm, concern for her evident both from his tone and his actions. 'You can lie down there and I'll get you some tablets.'

'No!' she'd shrieked. 'Er. Sorry. I don't mean to be ungrateful but I'd rather be alone if I'm going to be sick. Which I think I am. I've got tablets in my car. And bottled water.'

'You don't want to be sitting in a car feeling sick. Come to the pub. I'll get you settled and leave you be until you feel better.'

'Thanks. Really. But I'd rather not. Perhaps it's just delayed shock. You know? After nearly killing you earlier. Please don't worry. I'll be fine. I just want to sit by myself for a while.'

He looked unsure of what to do and the lines around his eyes expressed concern.

'At least let me help you back to your car then.'

'Thanks.'

She walked fast and virtually dived onto the seat.

'This feels wrong,' he said, leaning one arm on the roof and peering in the window. 'Please come into the pub.'

'I'll be fine. I'll see you later. I really need to go.'

She started the car and almost ran him over again as she crunched the gears and sped away.

Six

Mikkel watched in astonishment as Portia's car roared away from the car park.

What the hell had just happened?

Everything had been going so well.

Until he'd told her about his plans to buy Seahorse Harbour Holiday Park and build an eco hotel.

Did she have something against eco-tourism? She had said she enjoyed comfort but surely the mention of a self-sustainable hotel wouldn't make her feel sick? That was a bit far-fetched. Especially as she'd said she worked in tourism.

Perhaps it had simply been delayed shock. She'd definitely been shaking earlier but she'd clearly tried to hide that from him. Was she the type of woman who didn't like to show her vulnerabilities?

He didn't understand what had happened. Would he still be seeing her tonight for dinner? He didn't have her phone number and she didn't have his. He didn't even know her surname.

But he did know where she was staying.

What good was that? He could hardly turn up at Easterhill Hotel and Spa and ask for Portia's room number. There might be more than one Portia staying at the hotel – although it wasn't a common name so he doubted that would be the case.

But the hotel might require more than just her Christian name before giving out information. He could be a stalker or something for all they knew.

He could call and ask to speak to her. But again, they might require a surname before putting a call through to her room.

Or he could simply wait and see if she turned up at the restaurant. That was probably his wisest move. But 8 p.m. was twelve hours away. What was he supposed to do until then?

He cursed loudly and marched towards the pub.

What was wrong with him? He'd only known the woman for about ten minutes. What difference did it make if he never saw her again?

He knew the answer even as he asked himself that question.

It would make a lot of difference. Because as ridiculous as it may be, the last ten minutes had been the best ten minutes he had experienced for a long time.

Since before Diana had dumped him, in fact.

And that was another problem.

How did he feel about Diana?

Less than thirty minutes ago, he'd told her he thought he still loved her.

But surely, if he loved Diana, meeting Portia wouldn't have had such a strong impact on him?

And it had.

She had.

The moment he'd looked at her – really looked at her, it was as if he'd known she would be important to him. As if their meeting was meant to be.

And now that she was gone, it felt as if something was missing from his life.

This was insane.

He must be the one suffering from delayed shock. That must be it. It was the only explanation.

He pushed the pub door open and stomped inside. He was behaving like a love-sick teenager and he needed to stop this right now. He needed to find something else to concentrate his mind on.

He would work on the plans for his hotel. Seahorse Harbour Holiday Park had come up for sale far sooner than he'd anticipated and things were moving fast.

Not that it was officially on the market yet, and if he and the Turners, who owned the holiday park, agreed a price, it probably wouldn't go on the market at all. It definitely wouldn't be advertised until after the Easter holiday weekend.

The Turners had given him a heads-up because he'd expressed an interest in the site when he had first arrived in Seahorse Harbour.

At the time, the Turner family had no plans to sell, but they promised him they would let him know if things ever changed.

And recently, they had. Both Mr and Mrs Turner were celebrating their sixtieth birthdays this summer, in July and August, and after much deliberation they had apparently decided neither of them wanted to be running a holiday park in their sixties.

They had expected to pass the baton to their eldest son, but he and his wife had just declared they were moving to Australia, which was where the wife was from and where her family still resided.

The younger son wasn't keen to take the reins either. He'd met a girl in London and the bright lights of the big City beckoned.

Their daughter had never shown the slightest interest in the place, and being a late child who was only just eighteen, her eyes were fixed on uni and, having helped out at Asher Bryant's veterinary practice more than a few times over the last year, she had her heart set on becoming a vet.

The Turners battled with the idea of letting the holiday park go. It had been in Mrs Turner's family before she and her husband took over. But they couldn't force their children to run it, and they wouldn't have considered trying. They were firm believers in the adage that one must follow one's own star and lead the life one wanted. Their children's stars shone elsewhere, so the holiday park had to go.

The first person they had called, once they had made their final decision, had been Mikkel.

He'd confirmed he was still interested and suggested they get a valuation. He knew what the site was worth to him and he was aware of the market price for such a site, but he wanted them to know that the price he was willing to pay was a fair one.

The first person Mikkel had called, after breaking the news to his dad in Hell, had been Nathan Bromley.

Nathan worked at Seahorse Bites Café with his aunt Lyn now, but he was once an architect in a prestigious firm, and he and Mikkel had become good friends since Nathan had moved to Seahorse Harbour

49

permanently in January.

Mikkel had made that call just one week ago but Nathan had already drawn up some plans based on discussions they had had.

The plans needed a few tweaks here and there but they were definitely on the right track and Mikkel could already visualise his eco hotel on the site. It would consist of one main, large, pod-shaped building made from sustainable timber, and a number of much smaller pod-shaped structures made from the same timber dotted across the site. Some of these pods would face the sea while others faced the woodland that surrounded the site on three sides. Some pods were even built in Little Wood itself. A fairly large area of Little Wood was owned by Seahorse Harbour Holiday Park and was included in the sale.

Nathan and Mikkel had even placed a few of the pods in the trees themselves, but they weren't sure planning permission would be granted for those as the local authority might consider that a stretch too far. This was Seahorse Harbour Holiday Park after all, not an African safari park.

Nathan had drawn up two separate sets of plans and Mikkel would be holding preliminary discussions with the local authority before submitting his final plans for approval. That way he could get a feel for what the council might and might not be willing to grant approval.

Mikkel opened a locked drawer behind the bar and took out the folded plans he'd left there last night. He laid them out on the bar and smiled.

This was a dream come true. Even as a kid in Hell he'd dreamt of one day owning his own hotel. He'd worked in one as a teenager before moving to Oslo for a time and working in a bar.

But coming to England had also been a dream of his. His mum had been English and they'd holidayed in England several times. They'd come to Seahorse Harbour when he was about five or six and he'd thought the place was magical. That feeling had stuck with him despite holidays in more exotic locations and climes and that was why, when he'd heard through his grapevine of contacts that The Seahorse Inn in Seahorse Harbour was up for sale and also the old boatyard off the promenade, he'd decided to make the village his home and he'd jumped at the chance to buy them.

Adding Seahorse Harbour Holiday Park to his portfolio would be the culmination of his dreams. His dad had been almost as excited as he was when he'd called and told him the site was up for sale.

'I think it's time I paid you another visit,' Gray Meloy had said, after they had chatted about it for almost an hour.

'You're welcome anytime, Dad. You know that. And I suspect I won't be the only one who will be pleased to see you again. Elsie will be thrilled, I'm sure.'

'Elsie has her hands full, now that Lottie is living in the village. I still can't believe that all this time she had a daughter no one knew existed, but I'm pleased it's all worked out.'

'Asher's pretty pleased too,' Mikkel joked about his friend. 'Especially since he and Lottie got engaged.'

'Any news of his sister?'

'Sorcha hasn't been seen or heard from for over a month. But Asher did mention that his parents are coming to stay for a few days from Easter Sunday onwards and that Sorcha may be coming with them.'

'Are tongues still wagging about what happened?'

Mikkel laughed mirthlessly. 'Of course. This is a village. But something else will no doubt soon replace Sorcha's name on the gossiping tongues. And that may well be me, if people get wind of the sale of Seahorse Harbour Holiday Park and my proposed purchase and eco hotel.'

The pub door opened and Mikkel's head shot up from the plans.

Had Portia returned?

His smile faded as Diana stepped inside.

She looked beautiful, as always, but she also looked sad and lonely and confused.

'You didn't take my call.' Her lovely voice crackled with emotion.

Mikkel turned the plans over and moved away from the bar but he kept a safe distance between himself and Diana in spite of the fact that he wanted to wrap his arms around her and tell her everything would be okay. He couldn't do that though, because somehow, he wasn't sure it would.

'I'm sorry, Diana. I was busy. What are you doing here?'

She gave him a nervous smile.

'Can't a girl walk into a pub for a drink?'

'At 8 in the morning? Not really.'

'A coffee?'

He held her gaze.

'I don't think this is wise, Diana.'

'What has love ever had to do with being wise?'

That was true. Mikkel hadn't made wise choices when it came to love, and Diana hadn't either.

'Is that what this is? Love? I'm not so sure anymore.'

She looked stung by his words. He hadn't meant to hurt her. But sometimes you had to be cruel to be kind, didn't you?

'You said you loved me this morning.'

'I said I thought I did. I probably still do.

At least some part of me does. But I can't do this again, Diana. I told you that this morning. I don't want to sneak around. I want to have a relationship. A real relationship I can talk about openly. We can't do that if you're with Alex.'

'I might not be with him for much longer. I told you, Mikkel. Things have changed. I don't feel the same as I did.'

'Then make a decision.'

'It's not that simple. You said yourself, my kids need stability. Becca will be sitting her A levels over the next two months, and Toby – well, Toby was really shaken up by Alex's brush with death. He needs time.'

'And what about us, Diana? What about me? I have needs too. I need a woman I can trust. A woman who loves me. Do you love me, Diana? Really? Or am I just someone convenient to run to when things aren't going well with Alex?'

'That's not fair! Of course I love you. I told you that this morning. Would I be here, risking everything if I didn't?'

He shook his head and sighed.

'I don't know, Diana. I don't know anything anymore.'

She hurried towards him and he tensed involuntarily when she took his hand in hers.

'We were good together, Mikkel. You gave me the strength to tell Alex it was over.'

He snorted in derision.

'And yet you went back to him.'

'Yes. And I think that was a mistake. But I had to try. Don't you see that? Don't you understand? Not just for me but for the kids.'

'I understand that. What I don't understand is what's changed?'

'I told you earlier. I don't know. But something has.'

'And what if it changes again? What if we get back together and then, a few months from now, you decide you still love Alex, just like you did the last two times.'

'That's not fair. The first time with us just happened. I didn't plan it. I'd never cheated on my husband and I felt guilty, in spite of how he treated me and all of his affairs. I had to walk away from you. You must see that, surely?'

'Okay. I accept that. But then you said you wanted to be with me and to start a whole new life. A few months later, you were back with Alex. Why would this time be any different?'

'Third time lucky?'

'Is that some sort of joke?'

'No. Sorry. I ... I was just trying to make you smile. You used to smile all the time when we were together.'

'Not all the time. And I never smiled when we were apart.'

'We don't have to be apart, Mikkel. I want you so much right now I can hardly breathe. You still want me, don't you?'

Her hands slid beneath his jumper and he remembered what it was like to kiss her, to make love to her, to spend the day in bed with her. His hands moved to her hips and his fingers curled into the folds in her dress.

'Diana. Oh god, Diana.'

'Yes, Mikkel,' she whispered.

'No!'

It took every ounce of emotional strength to push her away. She looked as surprised as he was.

'Mikkel?' Her tone was strangled.

His own voice shook as he spoke. 'I ... I can't do this.' He stepped away from her and raked a hand through his hair. 'I told you that on the phone and I told you again just now. I mean it, Diana. You have to choose. You have to decide.' He let out a sigh and shook his head. 'And ... and I think it's only right to tell you. I ... I've met someone. Someone I think could mean a lot to me.'

'You've met someone? Who? When? You didn't mention that this morning. Are you ... are you sleeping with her?'

His laugh was almost pitiful to his ears.

'No I'm not. We've only just met. Today, in fact. So we haven't been on a date yet. I don't even know her surname. But I do know something happened to me when I met her. Something that has only ever happened to me once before. The day I first saw you.'

Diana gasped.

'You ... you told me once that you thought you fell in love with me the first time you saw me. Are you ... are you saying you think you've fallen in love at first sight with her?'

He shook his head. 'I don't know what I'm saying. You're not the only one who's confused. All I know is I felt something. Something special. And I've asked her to have dinner with me tonight. I don't know if she'll come. But I do know that I want her to.'

'Where does that leave me, Mikkel? Where does that leave us?'

'There is no 'us', Diana. Not while you're still with Alex.'

'And if I leave him?'

Mikkel met her gaze.

Would she? Would she leave Alex?

And even if she did, she'd left him before and look how that had turned out.

'Until you do, neither of us can answer that. I think you should go, Diana. We've both got a lot to think about.'

Seven

Portia's tummy was now rumbling almost as loudly as last night's storm. She needed something to eat – and fast.

But the only place open at this hour was the café Mikkel had told her about, and she couldn't go there, could she? He might have gone there on his own and she wasn't ready to face him again just yet.

It was only just 8 a.m. but this day was going from bad to worse. She had an hour to kill before her meeting and she had to eat before that. A growling stomach was hardly something you wanted when you were handling sensitive negotiations.

And these negotiations were going to need all the sensitivity she had. And all her ingenuity. But she would make the vendors aware that she knew another party was interested. She'd take the rug from under them and replace it with a magic carpet. Her magic carpet. They'd soon see hers was the only offer they would want to consider.

She'd done extensive research, not just about the site but also about the Turners. She knew everything about them. At least everything she needed to know to get this sale.

And she would get this sale. Not just for her but for her dad. He wanted this one more than he'd ever wanted any of the previous sites they'd bought. She wouldn't let anyone get in her way. Not even the handsome and charming, Mikkel Meloy.

But he was very handsome and extremely charming, wasn't he?

What was going through his mind right now? She had left him in a rather rude and odd manner. Was he cross? Was he confused? Was he wondering how she was, and where she was? Was he trying to imagine what she was doing at this moment?

Was he even thinking about her at all?

She was thinking about him, and that was irritating.

Her stomach rumbled again. She had to forget Mikkel, for now, and concentrate on finding food.

Hadn't he mentioned that Seahorse Harbour Holiday Park sold hotdogs? And pizzas? She sifted through her mind and remembered seeing them, and the ice cream parlour, and a bar during her research on the internet. They were all beside the pool, and that was near the entrance to the site.

She could go there. Surely something must be open for the holidaymakers staying at the holiday park? The owners wouldn't send their guests away from their own site when there was so much money to be made from food sales, would they?

She had been heading out of the village but now she turned the car around and drove back the way she'd come. She couldn't avoid passing the side of the pub, opposite the church, but at least she could avoid the frontage in Sand Lane, or the risk of being seen in Church Hill, by taking the longer route down Wood Lane instead. That led down to the seafront and the entrance to the holiday park itself.

She glanced briefly at the driveway leading to Mikkel's impressive home as she drove back down Seahorse Cliffs road, and her gaze wandered momentarily as she passed the pub, but thankfully, there was no sign of the man himself. She felt oddly disappointed.

She took in the view of the picturesque cottages in Wood Lane and gasped at the vista of the sea and horizon stretched out before her as she continued towards Sea Walk.

She could see the pool, or the Lido as it

was called as she drove towards the open gates of Seahorse Harbour Holiday Park. The infinity pool that would replace the Lido would be spectacular and the sweeping views across the bay would be magnificent.

Parking in a muddy car park left a lot to be desired, but she'd come prepared and had brought her wellies. She reached into the back and grabbed them from the footwell, slipping off her shoes and into the wellies before exiting her car. She was glad of them as her feet sank into the mud. It hadn't been this muddy at the top of Seahorse Cliffs. Which was lucky for Mikkel. Although he had been splattered all the same.

She tutted loudly. Why had she thought of him again?

The smell of bacon and sausages wafted towards her and she followed her nose which led her directly to Happy Hotdogs. It was little more than a kiosk really but the food smelt delicious, and it didn't just sell hotdogs, it seemed.

She was wrong. Hotdogs were the only things on offer, but there were bacon flavoured hotdogs, sausage hotdogs, mushroom hotdogs, steak and chips flavoured hotdogs. The list went on and on. How many additives and colours and unhealthy chemicals went into making those flavours didn't bear thinking about, but her tummy grumbled all the way there and right now, she was so hungry she would eat her own wellies if she had to.

A tall, dark and dangerously handsome looking teenager gave her a devilish smile.

'Good morning. What can I tempt you with today?' His voice was soft, soothing and somewhat sexy.

If she'd been eighteen and not thirty-six, a lot more than a chemical-filled, meat product.

'Er. What's good?' She returned his smile.

'Everything. And I'm not just saying that to make a sale. But the New York Weiner is possibly the best and the one I'd recommend.'

'That's what I'll have then. Thanks.' She watched him as he worked. 'You live in the village, I assume.'

He glanced over his shoulder.

'Actually I don't. I'm here from uni for the holidays and to spend time with my girlfriend, whose parents live here. She's also home for the holidays.'

'Is she at the same uni as you?'

He grinned mischievously. 'She's still at school. She's seventeen.'

'Oh, to be seventeen again. So you're just working here for a couple of weeks?'

He nodded. 'Yeah. I need the money. I

work here most holidays. My aunt works here full-time. She gets one of the caravans thrown in and I stay with her when I'm here.'

'Is it a good place to work?'

Again he nodded and his smile grew brighter. 'Yep. The people are great and the pay isn't bad, plus there're perks. Like free food, a pool and a place to meet the best girls. I met my girlfriend here last summer. I'm Noah by the way.' He pointed to his name badge.

'Pleased to meet you, Noah. I'm Portia.'

'Pleased to meet you, Portia.' He handed her the hotdog and pointed towards a row of various sauces. 'The New Yorker is the best sauce for this one, obviously.'

She slathered a spoonful of the spicy-smelling sauce across the hotdog and squeezed the bun tight before taking a bite. The last thing she needed was to get the thick brown sauce down her white blouse.

'Flipping heck! That's delicious.' She was genuinely astonished. 'And the sauce is the best I've ever tasted. I need to get that recipe.'

He winked at her. 'I think I can do that. I make it, so the recipe is mine.'

'You're a chef?'

'Not even close. But I do like cooking and inventing new recipes in my spare time. It's just a hobby though.'

'One you might want to consider

pursuing as a career if all your recipes are as good as this. And believe me, I know a thing or two about food.'

'What do you do then?'

'Oh. Er.' She hesitated for a second. But this guy was young and probably didn't even know the holiday park was being sold. 'I work for a large hotel chain. Trulove Hotels. Have you heard of them?'

His eyes opened wide. 'Hasn't everyone? Wow! I bet that's a fantastic job.'

She smiled at him. 'It has its perks.'

'What are you doing here then? Sussing out the competition?' He laughed loudly.

'Absolutely.' She laughed too. In some ways, that was the truth. Mikkel was competition. 'What's the pub in the village like? I'll be in the area for a couple of days and want to know where to go and where to avoid. Are there any decent restaurants?'

'Apart from this one, you mean?' He laughed again. 'The Seahorse Inn is great. And so is the guy who owns it. Mikkel Meloy. He's a friend of my girlfriend's family. Her name's Becca. Mikkel also owns Hippocampus on Sea Walk. It's a really upmarket place with prices to match but the food is second to none. He owns Neptune's nightclub too, if you like dancing.'

'I do. Very much. Thanks. I'll have to check all those places out.'

'Are you staying in the village? Other than here – and I don't think you're staying here, somehow; the only place is the Sunrise B&B. But even that's not the sort of place I can imagine you'd want to stay. Oh wait. Let me guess. You're at the Easterhill Hotel and Spa.'

'You're right. I am.' Portia grinned. 'But are you saying I don't look like the type of woman who could be happy in a place like this?'

'Could you?' He looked doubtful.

She laughed. 'Probably not.' She took another bite of her hotdog and closed her eyes. 'Although being able to eat these all day and night might tempt me. Is there a Ladies nearby? I've got to meet some people at 9 and I'd like to freshen up and clean my teeth beforehand.'

'Yep. Just over there to your right. I can get you a fresh, clean towel if you like.'

'That's very kind, but don't worry. A towel is something I always have in my car.'

He raised his brows in surprise. 'The loos here by the pool are fairly basic but they're spotless. My aunt makes sure of that.'

'Thanks.' She finished her hotdog in one more bite, wiped the sauce from around her mouth and tossed the paper napkin in the bin. 'I really enjoyed that. And I enjoyed our chat, Noah. I might see you again while I'm here, but if I don't, remember what I said about your hobby. Hobbies can often lead to fantastic careers. Good luck for the future.'

'Thanks. Good luck to you too. Enjoy your stay in Seahorse Harbour.'

She waved as she walked away. If he was open to the suggestion, she'd offer him a job in the new hotel she was going to build here. People like him were exactly the sort of employees that made a stay in a Trulove Hotel so perfect.

She made her way back to her car and took her towel, which was neatly folded in a zipped-up plastic bag, from the boot before making her way to the Ladies toilets.

Noah had described them perfectly. With white tiles on the walls and floors, three cubicles, three sinks, and a paper towel dispenser instead of a hot air hand dryer, they were fairly basic, but they were also spotless, just as he had said they would be. She would have to ask to meet his aunt. Assuming Portia liked her as much as she liked Noah, she would also offer his aunt a job.

She glanced at her reflection in the massive, rectangular, aged and faded mirror that took up almost one entire wall, and smiled.

'Way to go, Portia Trulove.' She laughed as she waved her arms in the air. 'You're already employing staff, and for a hotel that's not even built, on a site you don't yet own. Woohoo!'

She cleaned her teeth, splashed cold water on her face and reapplied her make-up, which consisted of merely lipstick and mascara. She had spent most of February on the island of St Lucia in the Caribbean, supervising the updating of the staff manuals at their Trulove Tropical Resort Hotel and Spa, and the sun-kissed glow of her tan was still apparent, so she didn't require foundation or blusher. She undid her ponytail, brushed her hair with the brush she always carried in her handbag, and tied her hair in another neat ponytail.

She returned her towel to the boot of her car, took off her leather jacket and replaced it with a more business-like midnight-blue suit jacket, and made her way to the office in Seahorse Harbour Holiday Park, just a few metres away from where she'd parked.

She had seen photos of the Turner family on the internet during her research, but Mr and Mrs Turner were not exactly what she had expected. They looked as they had in their photographs, but they sounded more like affectionate grandparents than astute business people trying to negotiate the highest price they could obtain for their property.

'You must be Portia Trulove,' Mr Turner said, hurrying towards her the moment she knocked on the half-open door. He shook her hand with one of his, whilst cradling their locked hands with the other. 'We're so sorry you've come all this way.' He gave her an apologetic smile and glanced at his wife who did the same.

'We did explain the situation to the estate agents,' Mrs Turner said, taking her husband's place as he moved to one side.

'We did,' he said. 'But they as good as insisted that you would still want to see the place, regardless.'

Portia looked from one to the other and managed a smile. 'I'm sorry. Am I missing something? You said "regardless." Regardless of what, exactly?'

The couple exchanged worried glances and tutted in unison.

'Don't you know?' Mrs Turner asked.

'Didn't the agents explain?' Mr Turner queried.

'Apparently not.' Portia smiled her friendliest smile. 'Let's start at the beginning, shall we? Are you telling me that Seahorse Harbour Holiday Park is no longer for sale?'

'Oh no, dear.' Mrs Turner beamed at her. 'It's still for sale.'

'Or perhaps not, strictly speaking.' Mr Turner shook his head at his wife. 'We've as good as agreed a sale. It's to someone in the village. We didn't really want to get estate agents involved, but our eldest son insisted it was the right thing to do, and even Mikkel advised us that it was wise for us to get a proper and independent valuation to ensure that he paid a fair price.'

Portia's mouth fell open and she snapped it closed. What was going on here? Was this their way of pushing up the price? It made no sense. Had the estate agents misled her and her dad? She would be having a few choice words with the estate agents later if so.

'Are you telling me you've already agreed to sell the property to Mikkel Meloy?'

'Yes, dear. Do you know him?' Mrs Turner seemed pleased at that prospect.

'We've met. Very briefly.'

This was unbelievable. No wonder Mikkel had seemed so sure of himself.

So the Turners weren't trying to orchestrate a bidding war. This was the estate agents doing. If the Turners sold the place to Mikkel, the agents wouldn't receive any commission. But if they introduced a purchaser who subsequently completed, they would. And the estate agents knew that if the Truloves were interested, a sale was as good as certain because they could outbid the majority of would-be buyers.

'He's such a lovely young man,' Mrs Turner was saying, clearly referring to Mikkel.

'Have contracts been signed and exchanged?' Portia asked, ignoring that comment.

Mr Turner shook his head. 'Not yet. We only decided to sell a couple of weeks ago, but even then we were still having doubts. We finally told Mikkel it was for sale just over a week ago.'

'And, may I ask if there is any reason why you would particularly want to sell to Mikkel Meloy?'

The Turners exchanged confused glances.

'He told us when he first moved here that he would like to buy the place if we ever decided to sell. Wasn't that so, my dear?'

Mrs Turner nodded. 'He did. And he lives in the village.'

'Is the purchaser living in the village of paramount importance to you?'

Again the confused glances passed between the Turners.

'Well … no. Not really.' Mrs Turner smiled warmly. 'But it would be nice to know that our holiday park is going to be taken over by someone local. It's been in our family for years, and in my family before that.'

'But he doesn't plan to run it as a holiday

park, does he? He's planning to replace it with a hotel.'

Mrs Turner nodded. 'Oh yes, dear. An eco hotel, whatever that is.'

'And that doesn't trouble you?'

'Should it?'

Portia smiled. 'No. But a luxury hotel would undoubtedly bring more money to the village. And more jobs.'

'More money to the village?' Mr Turner seemed to like that prospect.

'And more jobs, dear.' That was clearly important to Mrs Turner.

Portia beamed at them. 'I believe I can safely say that a Trulove luxury hotel would pay its staff a higher wage than Mikkel Meloy might be considering, meaning tourists and locals alike would all benefit.'

'Jobs are hard to come by in the village,' Mrs Turner said.

'And all the youngsters want to work in Easterhill, or even further afield, to gain better pay.' Mr Turner rubbed his chin between his forefinger and thumb. 'We hadn't considered that.'

'Perhaps it's something you might like to consider now,' Portia said. 'At Trulove Hotels, our staff are as important as our guests and we value them all alike. I have no idea what price you have discussed with Mikkel Meloy, but I obviously know the value the estate agents have put on the property. I also know your family has owned the site since the beginning, and it must be difficult to part with such a beautiful and well-run business. My father bought his first hotel with a massive loan when he was just twenty-one, and I know he feels the same way about his business as I'm sure you do about yours. We have considerable experience in the hotel industry, and whilst Mikkel Meloy I'm sure has some good ideas, this would be his first hotel. It would be such a pity if his ideas failed. And a disaster for everyone, especially the current staff and all the local residents if this wonderful site should fall into decline.'

'Goodness gracious!' Mrs Turner looked horrified, as Portia knew she would. 'That hadn't occurred to me for one minute.'

'His pub, restaurant and nightclub are all doing well,' Mr Turner said, but doubt was creeping across his brow. 'And his holiday rental is always full.'

'I'm certain that's all true,' Portia said, smiling warmly. 'But as someone who has worked in the hotel industry her entire life, from chambermaid to receptionist, to the position I now hold by my father's side, I can tell you from hard learnt experience that the hotel business is unlike any other. Now I'm not suggesting Mikkel Meloy wouldn't make a complete success of it. All I am saying is that I know how hard it is to do so. I have an idea. You said you haven't signed a contract yet, so why don't you both think about what we've discussed today and the worries and concerns the three of us all have, and perhaps we could talk again? Later this afternoon, perhaps? Or tomorrow? I've already fallen in love with Seahorse Harbour, so I'll be staying for a while. I can meet you again at whatever time and place, suits you.'

'That is awfully kind of you,' Mrs Turner said. 'You're so understanding.'

'I realise this is an extremely important decision for you both, and for your family's future, and I want to do my very best to help you make the right choice. Oh, and this may be presumptuous of me, but a little birdie tells me that you both have big birthdays coming up. One at the end of July and the other at the beginning of August. Is that correct?'

'That's the reason we've decided to sell,' Mr Turner said. 'We're not as young as we used to be, and our children have chosen to follow other paths, so there's no one in the family to take over the reins.'

'I understand. Well, this is just an idea, and please feel free to say no, but if you do decide you might like to sell to us, we would be more than happy for you both to spend a week or two at any of our hotels across the globe, so that you could see for yourself what a truly luxurious experience it is to be a guest at a Trulove Hotel. We can discuss all the details later, but do bear that in mind. I've taken up enough of your time for now. It was so good to meet you both and to have this opportunity to chat. I'm really looking forward to continuing our conversation once you've had time to consider all your options.' She handed each of them one of her business cards and smiled warmly as she shook their hands. 'I must confess, I've already had one of your delicious hotdogs and I'm truly impressed. I shall definitely be eating here again. Goodbye for now. Call me any time. Night or day. And if you have any questions or concerns, please feel free to ask.'

'It was lovely to meet you, dear,' Mrs Turner said, smiling enthusiastically. 'You're not at all what we expected.'

'I hope you are pleasantly surprised.'

Mr Turner beamed at her. 'We are, Miss Trulove. We truly are.'

'Please call me Portia. I feel as if we're already on our way to becoming friends.'

'Daphne and Samuel,' Mrs Turner said. 'Your father must be so proud to have such a kind, considerate and hardworking daughter, Portia. Goodbye for now, my dear. We'll have a chat with our children and call you as soon as we can.'

Portia breathed in the sea air as she virtually danced back to her car.

There would be a Trulove Hotel in Seahorse Harbour. She was as good as certain of it.

Eight

Portia had promised to call her dad the moment she had news. But in reality, there was no point in phoning him and giving him bad news. What could she say? That someone else was interested in the site and had almost clinched the deal, but that she had put a spanner in the works and was hoping for a result in her favour.

That was hardly news. At least not news that Tommy Trulove would want to hear. Unless he called her to see how things had gone, she would postpone contacting him until she had something concrete to say.

The Turners had said they would call her as soon as possible and she had no reason to doubt that. If they hadn't called her by the afternoon, that's when she would phone her dad and explain about the other interested party.

She may as well take a closer look at the village in the meantime. She could probably leave her car where it was parked. The place wasn't exactly packed. She took her notepad from her handbag, scribbled her mobile number on a page, along with a message saying, 'If you need me to move my car, please call me on this number. Thanks. Portia.' She tore off the note and stuck it under her windscreen wipers.

She strolled down the entrance road to the holiday park and turned left at the end. A steep wall dotted with spring flowers rose up to her left, forming the garden wall of a particularly picturesque, sunshine yellow cottage with a thatched roof, and a matching yellow chimney that puffed out cotton-wool-ball shapes of pale grey smoke into an otherwise clear, blue sky.

When she reached the driveway of the property, she peered into the front garden where a mass of flowers, shrubs and blossoming fruit trees nestled together. The cottage backed onto another area of Little Wood and she wondered if that area was included in the curtilage of the property. It would be interesting to know who owned this cottage. If they were interested in selling, it would add an extra twenty-five per cent of square footage to the site of the Seahorse Harbour Holiday Park.

Sea Walk and the beach were to her right and she marvelled at the circle of rocks that she had read formed the tale of the seahorse-shaped bay. The aerial photographs of the bay, which she had seen on the internet, did indeed clearly show the shape of a seahorse, the head of which had been almost opposite the spot where she had met Mikkel Meloy today.

As she walked along the promenade, she spotted a small row of shops. There was an ice cream kiosk called Nice Ice, currently boarded and shut up tight, no doubt only open once the weather had improved.

Across from that was a place called Beach Bakers. No doubt a bakery, which she confirmed as she approached. The window display was very jolly with shelves lined with fake grass decorated with plastic, frolicking lambs dressed with clumps of white wool, and bouncing, grey felt bunnies of various heights with cute faces and pointed ears that sat amongst rows of equally fake carrots.

The shelves also contained delicious-looking baked treats that were very real. Hot cross buns and Easter biscuits, several shapes and sizes of beautifully decorated Easter cakes, and so much more besides. Just looking at all those delights made Portia hungry again. The shelves were trimmed with rows of brightly-coloured bunting in the shapes of rabbits, lambs and carrots, and multi-coloured lights flickered on and off behind the pane of glass.

She had to go inside and buy something for later and as she pushed the door open and a tiny bell tinkled overhead, a woman in her late forties, Portia judged, threw her a welcoming smile.

'Be with you in a moment,' the woman said, whilst she continued tying a big yellow bow around a large, and scrumptious looking Easter Simnel cake.

'No rush. I can continue admiring your window display. It's delightful. And very tempting. It lured me in.'

The woman laughed.

'That's what I like to hear. I'm Bev. Are you here for Easter?'

'Just a few days, but I may decide to stay on for a few more. I'm Portia. Lovely to meet you.'

'Free spirit, eh? Lucky for some. I can't complain though. I love my bakery.'

'And rightly so. Everything looks amazing. Especially that white chocolate cake with the chocolate rabbits and, I assume, marzipan daffodils. But even I couldn't manage to eat all that, and as there's only me.' She shrugged and smiled.

'There's a mini version of that, if you're interested.'

'Interested? I definitely need one of those. Make that two. I'll buy one for a friend.'

'A real friend? Or a make-believe one, so that you can eat them both? Not that I'm judging. I had two for breakfast.' She rolled her eyes and laughed.

'I didn't think of that.' Portia laughed too. 'It's for a real friend. Although, we're not exactly friends. We've only just met.'

What was happening to her today? She'd only been in this village for a matter of hours and she'd already opened up to everyone she'd met far more than she would ever dream of doing, normally.

'Ooooh. That sounds intriguing. Male or female, may I ask?'

'Male.'

'Men love cake as much as we women do. Would you like it in a little box? I've got some in the shape of Easter bunnies. You have to lift their tails to open the box.'

'Yes please. That sounds like fun.'

'I'll put yours in one too. We all need a bit of fun in our lives. Oh dear. Speaking of fun... this isn't it.'

The door burst open and a beaming, buxom, ginger-haired woman with a mass of curls who was no taller than about four feet eleven and probably in her fifties, almost shoved Portia out of the way. Her face was rosy-cheeked and freckled and the tip of her nose was larger than the rest of it and turned up slightly at the end.

'Excuse me dear,' she said, with a distinctive Irish accent, her large and vivid green eyes looking straight past Portia. 'Bev! Have you heard the news? Now I'm not one to gossip, as you know, but I have it on good authority that Seahorse Harbour Holiday Park is up for sale and Mikkel Meloy is hoping to buy it.'

The woman waited for a moment for Bev to react, but Bev merely darted a smile at Portia and continued placing the two mini white chocolate cakes into bunny boxes.

'I'm with a customer, Lilith. I'll be with you in a moment.'

'Right you are,' Lilith said. 'Word is, he's planning to build some sort of eco hotel in place of the holiday park. Whatever that might mean. Goodness knows what an eco hotel is when it's at home, but there you are. That's what comes when foreigners move into the village. But I can see you're busy, Bev, so I'll pop next door and tell Lyn and I'll come back when you have more time to chat.'

She was gone faster than lightning and Portia couldn't stop herself from laughing even though the gossip had been a bit too close to home for comfort.

'Sorry about that,' Bev said, shaking her head and laughing. 'That was Lilith Shoe. If you want to know what anyone and everyone in this village is up to, she's the person to ask. But don't believe everything she says. Sometimes she gets the wrong end of the stick entirely.'

'You didn't seem that interested. Had you already heard that bit of gossip?'

Bev shrugged. 'Lyn might have mentioned something about it. She owns the café next door, Seahorse Bites. Her nephew is, or was, I should say, an architect. Although I suppose he's still an architect, he just doesn't work as one these days. Now he helps Lyn run the café. What was I saying? Oh yes. Um. I believe Lyn mentioned that Nathan helped Mikkel draw up some tentative plans. It's hardly a state secret though. The Turners, who own Seahorse Harbour Holiday Park, have been talking about the possibility for a couple of months. It's true that they only recently made a final decision but I'm surprised Lilith has only just found out.' She grinned wickedly before suddenly becoming serious. 'But then again, she has been busy gossiping about someone else for some time now. Oh dear. And now that I come to think about it, I believe I was the only person Lyn told about Mikkel's plans. And I've just told you, so that makes me a bigger gossip than Lilith. But you're just here on holiday for a few days so there's no harm done. Now can I get you anything else?

My chocolate and caramel hot cross buns are rather tasty.'

'I'll take two,' Portia said, more from feeling an odd pang of guilt than from a desire for a hot cross bun. But they did look tasty, there was no denying that. And she had no reason to feel guilty. Bev had volunteered the information. Portia hadn't asked.

Now she was in a rush to get away and to pop next door to see what else Lilith, the gossip had to say. And she wouldn't just be eavesdropping. She was dying for a cup of coffee.

She paid for her purchases, dropped the change in a jar on the counter top, marked, 'Help save our seahorses', and wished Bev a very happy Easter before hurrying next door.

Judging by the steamed-up windows, Seahorse Bites Café was clearly busy. Portia could hear voices and laughter through the closed entrance door, and the smell of bacon, sausages and freshly brewed coffee seeped out via the tiniest gap between the door and the frame.

Nothing smelt quite as good as bacon and sausages cooking, but it was only around 10.30 and Portia hadn't long ago eaten that hotdog, and now she had a cake and a couple of hot cross buns to eat later. They would no doubt last a day or two but cakes and buns were always better, fresh.

The large sign on the door made her stop to read it. There was a picture of a scruffy-looking dog and the sign stated, 'Dogs welcome, along with well-behaved humans'.

Lyn obviously had a sense of humour. Or was the sign the nephew's doing? It was aged and faded so it had clearly been there for some time.

Portia pushed the door open and another bell tinkled above her. They really liked little bells in Seahorse Harbour.

She glanced around for a vacant table and spotted one near a group of four women who looked to be of a similar age to her, apart from one. Three were probably in their mid to late thirties and one was much older but Portia wasn't sure by how many years. One was a beautiful blonde with an immaculate, shoulder-skimming bob, who looked a little like the very pretty woman sitting next to her with slightly longer, chestnut hair. The other two women had their backs to Portia, but turned briefly when she entered.

Portia squeezed past a couple of packed tables to get to the vacant one and the woman with the chestnut hair smiled up at her, before nudging the blonde and nodding towards the counter where Lilith was leaning against one end.

'I'm telling you, Lyn,' Lilith was saying. 'The place is up for sale.'

'I'm not disagreeing with you, Lilith. All I'm saying is maybe it is and maybe it isn't. Let's wait and see, shall we? We don't want to be blamed for spreading rumours, do we?' She craned her neck to look into the kitchen and lowered her voice, leaning closer to Lilith as she continued, but Portia could still hear her. 'Especially not after what happened with Sorcha. The poor girl hasn't shown her face in Seahorse Harbour since that all blew up and it's still a sensitive subject as far as Nathan's concerned. Talk can cause harm, Lilith.'

'The poor lad's still keen on her then?' Lilith shook her head but smiled suddenly. 'I may have good news on that front. I hear Asher's parents are coming to visit on Easter Sunday. Now as you know, I'm not one to gossip, but if the parents are coming, Sorcha's bound to come too. But maybe it's best not to get young Nathan's hopes up, just in case.'

'Good gracious. I hope she does. And if she does, I hope there won't be any further talk about her.' Lyn glared at Lilith.

'Everyone's forgotten all that, Lyn. Now all the tongues are wagging about the sale of the holiday park. And I have it on good authority that Mikkel's not the only one who wants the place. The Truloves are sniffing around. You've heard of them, haven't you? The ones of the hotel empire fame.'

Lyn stopped what she was doing and met Lilith's eye. 'The Truloves? I doubt that very much.' She tutted loudly and straightened a pile of menus.

Portia watched them surreptitiously while pretending to glance at her phone.

Lilith seemed peeved. 'Well, they are. Daphne Turner told me herself that she and Samuel are meeting one of them this very day. Imagine that. A Trulove Hotel in Seahorse Harbour.'

'I can't imagine that,' Lyn said. 'Tommy Trulove wouldn't bother with a place as tiny as this.'

Portia choked and quickly coughed to hide her astonishment. Did this woman know her dad? Or had she merely read about him and made an assumption?

'Are you, okay, love?' Lyn looked across at Portia, whose table was just a metre or so away, before shouting into the kitchen. 'Nathan? Can you hand me a glass of water, please?'

'I'm fine, thanks.' Portia tried to stop choking and coughing.

'Here.' The chestnut-haired woman at the nearby table leant back, half-turning, and handed Portia an unopened bottle of Coke. 'This might help.'

'Thanks,' was all that Portia managed between coughs. She took the bottle and smiled as best she could.

At the same time, Lyn hurried towards the table where Portia sat, carrying a glass of water that a good-looking guy in his thirties who was now hovering in the kitchen doorway, had handed her.

'Here's some water if you prefer, love.'

'Thanks.' Portia smiled again and drank the water before handing back the unopened bottle of Coke to the woman who had offered it to her. 'That was kind of you. Of all of you.'

Lyn grinned at her. 'Don't want anyone choking to death in my café. It might give customers the wrong impression. Are you okay now? Would you like some more?'

Portia shook her head. 'No thanks. I'm good. But I'd love a cup of coffee when you have a moment.'

'Coming right up. I'd ask if you want some cake, but I see you've been to Bev's.' Lyn winked at her and removed the empty glass from the table. 'Be back in a jiffy.'

Portia watched her walk away.

Did Lyn know Tommy? Was Lyn the 'she' he had let slip and quickly covered up? Or had Lyn, as Portia had thought a moment ago, merely read about him in a magazine and made assumptions?

It was difficult to tell Lyn's age, but she

was probably in her late sixties or maybe early seventies. Tommy was seventy-two.

And, in her youth, Lyn was probably a bit of a stunner. She had a cheerful smile, rosy cheeks, soft, warm blue eyes and tight blonde curls. Her body was a little on the cuddly side, but it was obvious that, beneath that bright yellow apron, there was once a shapely figure. Her voice was warm and friendly too and there was something else about her that made Portia think Lyn was the sort of woman Tommy Trulove might easily have made one of his many wives, if given a chance.

The woman with the chestnut hair glanced round again.

'Haven't seen you here before,' she said, smiling. 'I'm Josie. Are you on your own, or are you waiting for someone? I'm not being nosey. Well, I suppose in a way I am, but I was asking because, if you're on your own, you're welcome to come and join us.'

'Josie!' the blonde woman tutted, but she turned and smiled. 'Sorry. My sister thinks she should talk to anyone who is, or who seems to be, alone. Just ignore her.'

'That's fine,' Portia said. 'And no. I'm not waiting for anyone. I'm here on my own. But I don't want to foist myself into your group. Thanks for the offer though.'

One of the other women suddenly piped up: 'I came here on my own. Not today.

88

When I first came here at Christmas. But I did have my spaniel, Merry with me, and I was visiting a relative.' She beamed at the older woman by her side. 'Who turned out to be my mum. I live here now with my fiancé. He's the village vet.'

Josie rolled her eyes and tutted. 'Get to the point, Lottie. Are you still hungover from last night?' She laughed and the woman called Lottie grinned.

'I think perhaps I am. I can't seem to string a sentence together today. What I was trying to say was that I felt very alone when I arrived, but Asher, and you, Diana and Mum, and everyone else in Seahorse Harbour made me feel so welcome right away.'

'It does seem a very friendly place,' Portia said.

'It is,' the older woman said, smiling at Portia. 'I'm Elsie. Lottie here is my daughter, and Josie and Diana are my twin nieces.'

'Yep,' Josie said. 'We're all one big happy family. Move over, Di and let this young woman join us.' She smiled at Portia. 'Unless you'd rather not?'

Portia hesitated. She had never been in a situation like this before and wasn't sure what she should do. People here were exceedingly friendly. Or perhaps they were all a little weird. You didn't just introduce yourself to a total stranger and tell them your life story and invite them to join you. At least, she never would. Although since she'd arrived here, she had been divulging quite a bit about herself. Except the main facts. That she was a Trulove and here to buy the holiday park.

'I'd love to join you,' she said. 'I'm Portia.'

'Where are you staying?' Diana asked as she shuffled over and made room, albeit a little reluctantly it seemed.

'At the Easterhill Hotel and Spa. I arrived last night.'

'Having a spa break to reinvigorate the soul?' Diana persisted.

'Not exactly. I had some business nearby. I'm only staying for a day or two. This village is really beautiful. I saw a cottage earlier which took my breath away. It's sunshine yellow and sits on a bank opposite the bay. Do you...? Oh. You're all smiling. I was going to ask if you knew the owner but clearly you do.'

'I own it,' the older woman called Elsie said. 'I'm glad you like it.'

'I really do. I expect you've had lots of offers to sell it over the years.'

'Not one,' she laughed. 'But it's not for sale and never will be all the while I'm alive. And I plan to stay that way for many years to come.'

Portia could hardly ask the woman her age but Elsie was one of those women who clearly had a style entirely of her own and that added to the difficulty in judging how old she was. She was pretty, but had probably seen fifty several years before. Possibly even sixty. Her mass of wild grey curls with bright pink streaks and a purple fringe were all tied with a colourful scarf wrapped around her head. It was rainbow-coloured and had silver tassels with multi-coloured beads on each. Her tunic top looked long and covered much of the shin-length flowery skirt she was wearing, all beneath a well-worn, gentleman's cardigan that was several sizes too large for her. On Portia, that all would've looked a mess. On Elsie it somehow worked.

The daughter, Lottie was far less adventurous in her outfit. She wore jeans and a patterned jumper, as did Josie. Diana clearly had taste and style. Her grey trousers were designer and her cashmere jumper was the perfect tone of pale lilac to complement them. Her jewellery was expensive and with her immaculately styled hair and perfect make-up she could grace the cover of any magazine.

Portia had guessed Josie and Diana were related, but never that they were twins. Diana wore wedding, engagement and eternity rings on her third finger. Josie wore none. Lottie had said she had a fiancé and Portia spotted the beautiful ring. Elsie's fingers were bare, but her nails were every colour under the sun.

Spending a bit of time with these four women would be interesting and no doubt informative. Portia was desperate to ask if they knew Mikkel, but she couldn't come right out and say it, could she?

'You might decide to sell if someone builds a massive hotel right next door to your cottage,' Diana said to Elsie.

Elsie shook her head and smiled. 'That won't happen. The local council will never give permission. And strictly between us – and also you, Portia because you're with us and you don't know who Mikkel is anyway, Mikkel's already discussed his proposals with me. He wanted to give me a heads-up before anything was decided because the section of Little Wood included in the sale adjoins the area of the wood that backs onto my garden. I like his plans. In fact, I'd say they were a distinct improvement on the holiday park. Not that I've got anything against that, but some of the clientele of late, leave a lot to be desired, as we've all discovered for ourselves over the last two years.'

Portia had no idea what that was about. Had there been trouble at the holiday park?

She hadn't read about anything serious during her research.

But she was beginning to feel awkward and also rather deceitful. She hadn't lied to anyone here, or misled them, but by not telling anyone who she was, she was actually doing both, and as strange as it was, that was troubling her.

The problem was, having sat and listened first to Lilith and Lyn's conversation and then to this, if she now admitted that she was a Trulove and was here to buy the holiday park, with plans to build a luxury hotel, everyone would no doubt treat her differently.

She could at least admit that she knew who Mikkel was, couldn't she?

'Er. Actually, I do know Mikkel. Well, when I say I know him, I only met him this morning. I almost ran him down, in fact. He was standing in the middle of the road near the top of Seahorse Cliffs. Thankfully, I saw him in time, and he saw my car, and we both managed to take evasive action.'

Diana turned deathly pale. 'You ... you met Mikkel this morning?'

'Yes. And he mentioned the holiday park and his plans for an eco hotel. Although come to think of it, he did ask me to keep that to myself. But as you already know, it doesn't really matter.'

'Are you seeing him again?' Diana snapped.

Everyone around the table stared at Diana.

'Um. I'm not sure. He ... er ... he did invite me to have dinner with him tonight.'

'And are you?'

'Di!' Josie nudged Diana. 'Don't bite the poor girl's head off.'

Portia met Diana's look. The woman was clearly jealous. But she was married, wasn't she? Was something going on between Diana and Mikkel? Or was it merely wishful thinking on Diana's part?

'I'm not sure yet. I had planned to, yes. But ... something has come up and now I may have to cancel. The problem is, I don't have his mobile number. We just arranged to meet at his restaurant. Er ... I don't suppose one of you might have it and be willing to give it to me, would you? At least then I'd be able to let him know if I ... can't make it. I'd hate him to think I stood him up.'

'Di's got his number,' Josie said, giving her sister an odd look. 'I'm sure she'll give it to you. Won't you?'

Diana met Josie's eyes and hesitated.

'I've got it,' Elsie said, tutting.

Elsie proceeded to reel off the number, which Portia asked her to repeat as she keyed it into her phone, all the while aware of Diana

glowering at her.
What was that woman's problem?

Nine

No sooner had Portia keyed in Mikkel's number than the phone rang and her dad's photo icon appeared on her screen. He was no doubt calling for an update. She quickly hid the screen from prying eyes – namely Diana's – by holding the phone close to her chest, but she'd have to answer it. Or decline the call and phone him later. He might start to worry though.

'Excuse me,' she said, and quickly took the call. 'Hi. Sorry I haven't called. I'm in a café having a coffee and a chat with some lovely people.' Not that she'd got her coffee yet. 'Can I call you later?'

Tommy clearly understood that this wasn't a good time for a catch-up and he chuckled softly, as if he knew he might be overheard.

'Of course. I'll be here, waiting. Have fun, sweetheart.'

'I will. Speak soon. Bye.' She rang off and

put her phone away. 'That was my dad. We always end up having very long conversations, so it's best if I call him back.'

'No need to explain to us,' Josie said, grinning. 'I always try to avoid my mum's calls for as long as possible.'

'Here you are, love.' Lyn had brought the coffee. 'Sorry for the delay. It's a bit busy in here today.'

'No problem. Thanks.'

Lyn winked at her before smiling at the others. 'Can I get you lovelies anything else?'

'No thanks,' Josie said. 'Liam's probably waiting for me to give him a hand. He's asked me to help him rearrange the window displays for the Easter weekend rush.' She rolled her eyes before glancing at Portia. 'He's a ceramicist and he owns Fulbright Ceramics. If you're around for a day or two, pop in and say hello. The shop and workshop are both in The Olde Forge, opposite the church. You can't miss it.'

'He made that gorgeous seahorse,' Lyn said, pointing to the statue taking pride of place in the café. 'He's exceptionally talented.'

'That's why I love him,' Josie said, beaming with pride. 'And because he's also extremely hot, sexy and wonderful.' She got to her feet. 'But sometimes I wish his work wasn't in such demand. I swear he's spent more time at his potter's wheel this week than he has with me. I'm beginning to think he prefers it to me.'

'I don't believe that for a minute,' Elsie said, laughing. 'The man is mad about you. He used to take his work far more seriously than he does now and he was always working. He's so much happier than he was when he was working in the City. But since you two have been together, he's been living on cloud nine.'

'Yes. That's what Orla says. Oh. Orla's Liam's daughter, Portia. It's a long story so I won't go into details but his wife died a few years ago and Liam and I got together when I came to stay with Di for the holidays last summer. We'd known one another since we were kids but I hadn't seen him for years. He worked in London for a long time but he changed careers after Una's death.'

'Tragic or other major events often make people reassess their lives. Or act completely out of character,' Portia said.

Josie, Diana, Lottie and Elsie all exchanged odd glances and Portia remembered how her own mum's death had made Tommy react. He'd never been unfaithful, as far as Portia knew, but suddenly all he wanted to do was chase younger women. It was his way of coping with losing the one woman he truly loved.

'Yes,' Josie said, giving Diana a pointed look. 'There's been a lot of that around here. People reassessing their lives, or acting completely out of character.'

A wave of colour flushed Diana's face. 'I'd better go too. I've got things to do.'

'We'd better make a move soon as well, I suppose,' Elsie said to Lottie, before smiling at Portia. 'We're going clothes shopping in Easterhill. I wanted to drive my moped but my daughter here says we need to take a cab because there won't be enough room for all our bags.' She laughed. 'I think it's going to be a long day.'

'I need some new clothes,' Lottie protested, laughing too. 'And you were the one who suggested a cab when I told you what I wanted. I was perfectly happy to shop online.'

'What's wrong with your car?' Josie asked Lottie.

'Nothing. Mum said a cab will mean we don't have to worry about parking. It is the Easter holidays, after all.'

'The shops will be manic,' Diana said. 'Rather you than me.'

Lottie nodded. 'I know. But Lilith told me there's a new bridal shop opening in Easterhill today so that clinched it. I want to pop in there.'

'Is there?' Josie sounded interested. 'You

didn't tell me that earlier. I might've come with you if I'd known.'

'You can still come with us,' Lottie said.

'I can't. I need to help Liam. Although … I'm sure he wouldn't mind. And we can move the displays around later. I'll give him a call and ask.'

Diana looked confused. 'Why are you so eager to look in a bridal shop? Is there something you're not telling us? Are you and Liam planning to get married?'

'I bloody well hope so.' Josie nudged Diana's arm. 'But no. We haven't discussed marriage. Not in so many words, at least. We both want to one day though. I'd marry him tomorrow if he'd ask me.'

'You could ask him,' Elsie said.

Josie tutted. 'No way. I want the romantic proposal. I was sort of hoping that Asher and Lottie getting engaged so soon might spur Liam on. But I think all that stuff with Una might have put him off marriage a bit. And we are blissfully happy as we are, so I suppose there's no rush.'

'So why do you want to go to a bridal shop?' Diana persisted.

'Because you never know, do you? And besides, I like to be prepared. Why don't you come too? It might cheer you up. You've been miserable all morning.'

'I've got a lot on my mind. And a bridal

shop is the last place I want to be today, thank you.'

'What is wrong with you today? Has something happened? Oh God. Alex isn't up to his old tricks again, is he?'

'No! Of course not.'

'Okay. Don't get stroppy. Are you having doubts again?'

Diana shot a look at Portia.

'I don't want to discuss it at the moment. This isn't the right time or place.'

'Er. Is there something to discuss? I don't have to go shopping. Or help Liam if you need to have a talk, Di.' Josie reached out her hand and squeezed Diana's arm.

Diana mellowed instantly. 'No. It's fine. It can wait. I've got some thinking to do, that's all. We'll have a chat about it soon.' She darted another look at Portia. 'Besides, I need to see how things go this weekend.'

'What's happening this weekend then?' Josie asked.

'Stop asking so many questions,' Diana said, smiling wanly before looking Portia directly in the eye. 'I'll say goodbye, Portia. I don't suppose we'll be meeting again as you're only here for a day or two. You are only here for a day or two, aren't you?'

How odd that she repeated that. As if to emphasize the fact.

'Now who's asking questions?' Josie

laughed.

Portia smiled. 'Yes. That's the plan. It was lovely to meet you, Diana. It was lovely to meet you all. Have fun shopping.'

'Don't forget to pop in to The Olde Forge, if you have time,' Josie said. 'Tell Liam you met me here, if I'm not around when you come by. Which reminds me. I said I'd give him a call didn't I, and tell him I'm going shopping?' She waved at Portia and also said goodbye to Lyn as she took out her phone and she and Diana walked towards the door.

'Bye, Portia,' Lottie said as she and Elsie also got up to leave.

'Enjoy your stay,' Elsie said, leaning closer and lowering her voice so that only Portia could hear. 'And if I were you, I'd keep that dinner date with Mikkel. He's a genuinely decent guy and he deserves to meet a woman who could make him happy.'

'Oh! Er. It's just dinner. Nothing could come of it. I'm only here for a couple of days. And I'm not looking for a relationship. Besides, it's ... it's all a bit complicated.'

'Love often is, but sometimes it's worth making an effort for.'

'Love? This has nothing to do with Love. We've only just met.'

Elsie smiled, winked and walked away without another word.

Ten

Several times throughout the day, Portia took out her phone, selected Mikkel's number and considered calling him to cancel their dinner plans, but each time something stopped her.

She did eventually call her dad. It was just before 1 p.m. and she was trying to decide where to go for lunch.

She could return to Seahorse Harbour Holiday Park and have another scrumptious hotdog. But if the Turners saw her there, they might think she was being a little pushy.

There was The Seahorse Inn. But that was Mikkel's pub and there was a chance he might be there. She wasn't ready to come face to face with her competition just yet. He also owned the only restaurant in the village, so Hippocampus was out.

That only left two options. She could drive back to Easterhill where there were plenty of cafés and restaurants to choose from. Or she could go back to Seahorse Bites Café.

She decided on the latter, which reminded her to call her dad.

'Sorry I've been so long. I've been meeting some of the residents.'

'Mixing business and pleasure, eh?' Tommy chuckled. 'You've always had a knack for that. Did you learn anything to our advantage?'

'Yes and no.'

'Hmm. First tell me how the meeting went. How long will it be until they sign the papers, do you think?'

'Er. About that, Dad. It might not be quite that straightforward. It seems we weren't the first to hear the holiday park was for sale. We have competition and the guy is local. He owns the only pub, restaurant and nightclub in the village and the Turners were surprised I still wanted to meet them as they'd told the agents the holiday park was as good as sold.'

'Sold? How can that be? The agents only gave us the heads-up a few days ago.'

'Yes. And I'm going to have a word with the agents later. I'm not keen on surprises like that.'

'Are you telling me we're out of the running?'

'Not exactly, no. I think I might have given the Turners pause for thought. I definitely gave them a few things to consider. Oh, and I dangled a free holiday in front of them as a sweetener.'

Tommy breathed an audible sigh of relief.

'That's my girl. We're back in with a chance then?'

'I think so, yes. They're going to call me once they've had time to reconsider their options and I've got a feeling they'll say they want to have further discussions. They seem like decent people and they'll feel bad even thinking about letting the other guy down. But they're also realists, I believe, and they'll realise this is the only chance they'll get to sell the place. They've got adult kids who'll probably have something to say about it too. I think they'll all see we've got far more to offer them than Mikkel. Er. He's the local guy. Anyway. I'll do my best. And I'm feeling pretty positive, all things considered.'

'I'm pleased to hear that. I'd hate to lose out on this deal. What else do you know about our competition? This Mikkel guy.'

'A little. I actually met him by accident this morning. I'll tell you about that another time but let's just say, he's invited me for dinner but he doesn't know who I am.'

'Really? That could be interesting.'

'That's one word for it. If he finds out my identity before tonight, it could also be a car crash.' She laughed at that. 'And that's sort of how we met. I nearly ran him over this morning but thankfully we both took evasive action.'

'You're joking?' Tommy laughed too but quickly became serious. 'You're not joking, are you? Were you hurt?'

'Not at all, Dad. Don't worry.'

'I'm your father. I can't help but worry. It goes with the turf. Any damage at all?'

'None whatsoever.'

'That's a relief. Where are you having dinner?'

'At his restaurant. It's called Hippocampus if you want to check it out on the internet.'

Tommy chuckled. 'You know me so well, sweetheart.'

'I do.' She hesitated for a second. 'Dad? Do you know a woman called Lyn? I don't know her surname but she owns a café on the promenade. It's called Seahorse Bites Café and it's on Sea Walk. Dad? Are you still there?'

Tommy coughed. 'Is she blonde and blue-eyed with a cheerful smile and a personality to match?'

'That's her to a tee. So you do know her?'

'I did. Yes. Many years ago.'

'Did you ... did you date her?'

'I did. Yes. It was before I met your darling mother. In fact, it was Lyn who introduced us.'

'You're kidding! You met Mum in Seahorse Harbour! You never told me that. Why didn't you mention it when we heard about the holiday park?'

'I honestly don't know. I should've I suppose. But it was all so long ago.'

'That explains why the place is so special to you. I wish you'd told me. Ooooh! I could've even used that in my purchase bid. Everyone likes a good romance. And saying the place is dear to us because it's where you met Mum would've added extra oomph. Or is that why you didn't tell me? You didn't want Mum to become part of my pitch?'

Tommy let out a soft sigh. 'As I said. You know me so well. But it wasn't quite so romantic when we met.'

'Will you tell me about it now, Dad? I do remember you and Mum saying you met on holiday, but I don't remember it being at an English seaside resort. I thought it was abroad. And I don't recall hearing about Seahorse Harbour. I think that name would've stuck in my mind.'

'It's because, although we first met in Seahorse Harbour, we were both dating other people. I was dating Lyn. Your mum was dating … Lyn's future husband.'

'What? No! Are you saying you and Mum cheated on your partners and got together?'

'Not us. No.'

'Not you? Oh God. You mean Lyn, and Mum's then boyfriend, cheated on you two?'

'Yes. Which is why Seahorse Harbour means a lot to me. It was the scene of one of the worst periods of my life, but ultimately it led to the best period of my life. The best and happiest of times, in fact.'

'What happened? Do you mind talking about it?'

He let out another sigh. 'It brings back a lot of memories. I'm not sure discussing it over the phone is the best way to do it. Why don't we wait until you're back? We can talk about it properly, face to face.'

'Of course. If that's what you'd prefer. But can I just ask one thing?'

'Ask away.'

She heard the tension in his voice. This was definitely a tender topic, even after all these years.

'Did Lyn break your heart? Is that why you and Mum got together? And did Mum mend it? I know that's three things. Sorry.' She gave a small laugh to lighten the moment.

'Yes. Lyn broke my heart, and yes, your mum definitely mended it. But not right away. We were both heartbroken at the time. That's why we always said we met on holiday in Italy. We both wanted to forget what happened to us in Seahorse Harbour. And it was almost two years later that we bumped into one another again, but we recognised one another instantly. It wasn't love at first or even second sight though. We became friends. It wasn't until I almost lost your mum to someone else that I realised how much I loved her. And before you ask. Yes. I did love your mum far more than I loved Lyn. And I never stopped loving her until the day she died. No. That's not true. I never stopped loving her. Even now. I don't think I ever will. Your mum was the only woman I've ever truly loved. Apart from Lyn, for a while. And you and Bethany of course, but obviously, that's a different kind of love.' He laughed suddenly. 'So much for waiting to discuss it face to face.'

'Wow, Dad. Thank you for telling me.' She hesitated for a second. 'That's why you keep getting married, isn't it? You're still trying to block out the pain of losing Mum, aren't you?'

Tommy gave a heartfelt sigh. 'And making a complete and utter mess of it. She would laugh at me, you know, if she were alive to see the way I've been behaving. But then if she were still alive, I would be a happily married man and wouldn't so much as look at another woman. But as I said. Not really a conversation to have on the phone. When do you expect to be back?'

'Oh. Er. Easter Sunday, perhaps. That gives the Turners the rest of today and all of Friday and Saturday to think things through. If that's the case, let's have Sunday lunch together. You, me and Bethany.'

'That sounds perfect. We'll hope to see you on Sunday. Wait. Portia? Does Lyn know who you are?'

'No. Only the Turners, so far. But I'm going to the café for lunch and I'm feeling a bit odd about keeping my identity under wraps. It's really weird, but I feel as if I'm being deceitful somehow. I've never had this feeling before. It's very strange.'

He snorted down the phone. 'Lyn will tell you it's the seahorses. She used to say they were magical or some such thing. Unless she's changed. Which I doubt very much. She said they brought out the best in anyone who visited the village, and they made people tell the truth. All nonsense, of course.'

'Especially if she cheated on you. That was hardly truthful, was it?'

'Actually. It was. They fell in love at first sight, so they said, and they told your mum and me within a day of them admitting their feelings to one another. But I'll tell you the full story when I see you.' He laughed suddenly. 'Watch out for those seahorses and their magical powers. You might find yourself telling everyone the truth. And sometimes the truth isn't always what people want to hear.'

Tommy was right about that. Portia was dreading Mikkel hearing the truth.

Eleven

'Back so soon, love?' Lyn beamed at Portia as the little bell tinkled over Portia's head. 'Is it our coffee or our charm that's brought you back?' She gave a little laugh and pointed to a table in the window. 'I'd grab that one while it's free. Best view of the bay from there.'

'Thanks. And it's a bit of both, I think. And the wonderful aromas wafting through the door. I could smell something delicious from around the corner.'

'Ah. That'll be our Easter roast. I can highly recommend it. But then I would, wouldn't I? Sit yourself down and I'll bring you a menu in a jiffy.'

Portia made her way to the table. The café wasn't quite so packed as it had been, which was a surprise as it was gone 1 p.m. now. Perhaps people ate lunch early in Seahorse Harbour.

Lyn must've read her mind.

'You've missed the peak lunchtime rush. People were queueing at the door an hour ago.' She handed Portia a menu and took her pad from the pocket of her yellow apron. 'Have you had a good look around the village?'

'I've been to the church. It's beautiful inside and out. I'm not religious but I do love churches. I've got a bit of a thing about all buildings, actually.'

'You and my nephew should get together. He's an architect by profession and buildings are like goddesses to him. He's given it all up for a time to come and help his poor old aunt. Who, by the way, is neither poor nor old. Well, perhaps I'm not as young as I once was, but there's life in this old girl yet, let me tell you. Our burgers are good too, if you like them thick and meaty. Or our lunchtime toasties. They're very popular. What else have you seen? The Weeping Eye mustn't be missed. But that's up on Seahorse Cliffs on Seahorse Point. Don't go too near the edge though. The sea's still rough and when the tide's in, a spout of water shoots up from a cave through a hole on top of the cliffs. It's impressive in any weather but on a day of rough seas, it's also a bit dangerous.'

'I've read about that. I haven't seen it yet though. I'll take a look on my way back to Easterhill this afternoon.'

'Oh yes. I forgot you're staying there. That's the problem with the village. It only has a couple of places for tourists to stay. Seahorse Harbour Holiday Park, Sunrise B&B and The Boathouse. Not one of those is very luxurious.'

'So a luxury hotel here would be a good thing, in your opinion?'

'A luxury hotel? Oh. You were here when we were discussing Mikkel's plans, of course. But Mikkel wants an eco hotel so I don't think that would be particularly luxurious either.'

'What about a Trulove Hotel?'

'A ... Trulove Hotel?' Lyn paused for a moment before shaking her head. 'Don't believe everything you hear Lilith Shoe say, love. I don't think that will ever happen.'

'You might be surprised.'

Lyn eyed her curiously. 'Oh? Do you know something the rest of us don't then?'

Portia leant forward, her forearms resting on the table. 'I haven't been completely open. I haven't lied to anyone. I just haven't ... well. I've held back certain things. Like my surname, for one. Please don't be cross. I wasn't trying to be deceitful. I simply didn't want to cause an uproar.'

Lyn's eyes narrowed. 'And why would you cause an uproar? Unless you're here representing the Truloves and Lilith was right. She said one of the Truloves was here today. So that would mean ...' Her voice trailed off and her mouth hung open.

'I'm Portia Trulove. Tommy Trulove's eldest daughter. I believe you knew my dad.'

'Well blow me down and paint me yellow! You're Tommy's girl?' A huge smile swept across her face. 'I knew him long ago, love. Tommy was a good-looking lad, let me tell you, and he had a heart of gold. He also had a head for business and was determined to make his millions. I always knew he'd be rich and successful one day. How is he? I heard his wife died several years ago. I knew her too. Briefly. We both worked in this café one summer. That was a lifetime ago now. Oh bless my soul. That would've been your mum. So sorry, love. I also heard Tommy's been married a few times since. He doesn't seem happy. Or am I misjudging the situation?'

'He's happy in most ways, but not where love is concerned. Mum was the love of his life and he's still mourning her. We all are. I have a younger sister too. But it's worse for Dad on so many levels. They did everything together and although Mum's been gone for a long time now, he's often told me it still feels like only yesterday. Anyway. I recently discovered that they first met here. In Seahorse Harbour.'

Lyn coughed and adjusted her apron. 'Yes. They did.'

'And that you introduced them.'

Another cough. 'I believe I did. It was all so long ago now. So it's true then? He's considering buying the holiday park and building a Trulove Hotel? That's a surprise. I can't see the planners agreeing to that. They're very strict about what can and can't be built here. And we have the seahorses to consider. They're protected. A luxury hotel wouldn't be good news for them. I'm sorry to put a spanner in his plans but I think he's backing a losing horse this time.'

'We've taken the seahorses into consideration. And this hotel won't be like our others. Not in size, at least. We're planning something far, far smaller. In fact, it'll look more like the palatial Roman villa that once stood in the bay. I know there's hardly any of that remaining now and the entire site is under water about a mile or so out because the sea has eroded the coastline over the centuries, but there's good evidence of what the villa looked like and we've based our plans on that. From what I know of the local authority, a replica of that villa would prove popular. And it would provide yet another tourist attraction to Seahorse Harbour. Not to mention the fact that we would contribute a substantial portion of the profits to local projects and charities, especially the village's very own 'Save the Seahorse' ongoing campaign.'

Portia might have only just discovered Lyn's connection to her dad, but one thing she already knew was that everyone who ran a business in this village contributed something to the Save the Seahorse fund. Anything that generated money for that was bound to get a thumbs up from the locals. Even a luxury hotel.

Mikkel's eco hotel couldn't do that. Could it?

Or maybe she was underestimating Mikkel Meloy. From what she'd seen of him so far, he was a pretty impressive man.

'Really?' Lyn said, but she didn't look entirely convinced. 'We'll have to see about that, won't we? Now what can I get you to eat?'

'I'll have a cheese and ham toasty, please. And a pot of tea. And, if you have some time, I'd love to hear more about you and my dad.'

Lyn's brows furrowed. 'I'm not sure there's that much to tell. Best ask Tommy about that.'

'I have. But I'd love to hear all about it from you, too.'

'Would you indeed?' She smiled but it looked forced. 'Sometimes the past is best left where it is, love. It was all so long ago. I'm not certain I really remember what happened way back then. People come into our lives and people go. That's just the way it is. I'll get you your tea. The toasty will be ready in just a jiffy.'

Clearly Lyn didn't want to dig up the past. Was she feeling guilty about the way she and her husband treated Portia's parents all those years ago?

Twelve

Portia made two decisions. No matter what, she would meet Mikkel for dinner. And for that, she would need to buy a new dress.

She'd only brought a few things with her and none was suitable for dinner with an extremely attractive man. Especially not in a restaurant like Hippocampus. When she'd checked it out online, she'd been pleased to see it wasn't that different in style to a Trulove Hotel restaurant. Trendy but tasteful inside and out. Some tables were brightly lit with expensive, glass pendant shades, for those having business or formal dinners, while some tables were tucked away and dimly lit to provide a romantic ambience.

Which table would Mikkel choose for their dinner?

And why was she hoping it was tucked as far away from prying eyes as possible?

She was still mulling over her conversations with her dad and also with Lyn as she wandered from store to store in Easterhill shopping centre, so she didn't spot the three women walking towards her. But she did recognise the voice.

'Well, well,' Josie said, in a none too friendly manner. 'If it isn't Portia Trulove. Fancy seeing you here. Are you planning on buying the shopping centre too? Or is that something else you're going to keep from us?'

'Now, now, Josie,' Elsie said, in soothing tones. 'Try to see things from Portia's point of view.'

'She still should've told us who she was.' Lottie sounded equally as peeved as Josie.

'Ah.'

Portia couldn't think of anything else to say at first. How had they found out?

'Ah?' Josie glared at her. 'We tell you all about Mikkel and all you say is "Ah". Don't you think we deserve some sort of explanation? And an apology too. We were being friendly. You, on the other hand, clearly weren't.'

'I'm so sorry, Josie. And Lottie and Elsie. And you're right. It probably seems as if I was behaving like a bit of a bitch. But you must understand that there was no way I was going to open up about who I was when Lilith and Lyn were already discussing the reason why I was in Seahorse Harbour. If I'd said, 'I'm Portia Trulove and I'm here to buy the holiday park', everyone would've been asking questions and giving their opinions. All I wanted was a cup of coffee. Not an interrogation. But yes. I can see why you're annoyed.'

'And hurt,' Lottie said.

'Are you sure you just wanted coffee?' Josie asked. 'Not information?'

Portia shook her head. 'Mainly coffee. But if I'm being honest, I did want to know what people were saying about the sale of the holiday park. It's all supposed to be confidential but it seems it's anything but.'

'Few people can keep a secret for long in Seahorse Harbour,' Elsie said.

'You did.' Josie grinned suddenly.

Elsie shrugged and grinned back. 'I'm good at keeping secrets. You should know that.'

Josie nodded. 'That's true.'

Portia had no idea what they were referring to but it had nothing to do with her.

'I am sorry. Honestly. But this is business. It's what I do for a living. And we tend not to want everyone to know what we're planning until the deal is done.'

'Mikkel probably feels the same.' Josie met Portia's eyes.

'Perhaps. But he told me himself about his plans and I was a complete stranger. That's not something I would usually do.'

'That's because he's open and honest and trusting. Plus, he doesn't have a deceitful bone in his body.'

If Josie had slapped Portia's face, it couldn't have stung more than those words.

'I owe him an apology too.'

'You bet you do. But you might find dinner tonight is off.'

'He knows?'

Josie nodded. 'He does. And I believe I can say without hesitation that he wasn't thrilled about it.'

'No. I don't suppose he was.'

'At least you had the decency to tell Lyn who you were.' Josie seemed to have mellowed a fraction. 'But unfortunately for you, she told Nathan, who, of course, called Mikkel, who then called Liam. Nathan had told Mikkel that we were all sitting with you in the café and Mikkel asked Liam if I'd mentioned you at all. You can imagine my surprise when Liam then called me.'

'Yes. I can.'

'I had to call Mikkel and tell him that none of us had the faintest idea that you were Portia Trulove of the Trulove Hotel empire fame. That made him more cross than he had been already.'

Portia sighed. So much for the new dress she'd just bought.

'There's not really much I can say. Apart from, once again, I'm sorry. But business is business and I can't apologise for that.'

'So you're sorry, but you're not?' Josie looked confused.

'Yes. I like you all. I really do. And at any other time, I would've happily told you who I was. But as I explained, I wasn't prepared to be the centre of gossip and speculation when all I wanted was a coffee. And, as I admitted, to hear if there were any rumours going around. Which there were.'

Elsie smiled comfortingly and nodded. 'I think I probably would've done exactly what you did, if I were in your shoes. As would you, Josie. I'm pretty sure of that. But not you, Lottie, darling. You would've told everyone who you were, regardless. And that's another thing I adore about you.'

'I don't like secrets,' Lottie said. 'But I've learnt that sometimes people keep them for what they believe to be the right reasons, even if they're not.'

Portia had no idea what that meant but chose not to ask.

'Well, I think we've cleared the air,' Elsie said. 'Why don't we all go and have a nice glass of wine?'

'Good thinking,' Josie smiled. 'I could murder a glass of red.'

'Me too,' Lottie said. 'And I need to sit down. My feet are suddenly killing me. I knew I should've worn my trainers.'

'It was lovely to see you again,' Portia said. 'And once more. I am truly sorry for misleading you all. Enjoy your wine.'

'Aren't you joining us?' Elsie asked.

'Oh!' Portia glanced at each of them in turn. 'I hadn't realised I was invited. Aren't you all cross with me?'

'Yes,' Josie said, but she was grinning. 'Which is why you're buying the wine.'

'And telling us all you feel able to divulge about your plans for the holiday park,' Elsie added.

'And how you're going to apologise to Mikkel,' Lottie said. 'Because he deserves an apology too. In fact, more so than the rest of us.'

'I'll happily buy the wine. As much as you can drink. And I'll tell you about our plans for the holiday park. But as to how I'm going to apologise to Mikkel, I haven't a clue. I think that's something I may need your help with.'

'There's a rather nice wine bar just around the corner,' Elsie said. 'It's the one we always go to when we come to Easterhill, shopping.'

'Lead the way,' Portia said.

People from Seahorse Harbour really were rather weird. One minute they're all cross with you, the next they're inviting you for drinks – albeit at your expense. Perhaps she could offer to pay for dinner tonight and hope that Mikkel would be as quick to forgive her as Josie, Elsie and Lottie seemed to be.

But what was really weird was that she felt she had something she needed forgiveness for. She'd only done what she always did when trying to acquire a site for a Trulove Hotel.

And she'd never, ever felt one iota of guilt about it before.

Thirteen

Mikkel looked stunned as he opened his front door at 7 p.m. that evening.

'Portia! What are you doing here?'

Portia held up the cake she'd bought for him in Beach Bakers, still in the bunny box with a beautiful bow tied by Bev, together with an exceedingly expensive bottle of wine.

'I come bearing gifts.'

Having merely glanced at the bottle of wine, he stared dumbfounded at the box which was dangling from Portia's fingers and twirling slowly in the evening breeze.

'Gifts? You think gifts will change the way I'm feeling right now?'

'I was hoping they might help. The cake is delicious. I had one earlier. And the wine is exceptionally good.'

'Cake and wine. Seriously? You lied to me about who you were and why you were here and you think cake and wine will make up for that?'

'Firstly, I didn't lie to you. I told you my name is Portia, and it is.'

'Fine. But you said you were here on holiday.'

'No. You assumed I was. I said I was here for a couple of days on business and pleasure. Which is true.'

'You said you were in the tourist industry.'

'I am. The hotel business is part of the tourist industry.'

'Why didn't you just say you were the daughter of a hotel magnate? I'll tell you why. Because then I might've guessed you were in Seahorse Harbour because you'd heard Seahorse Harbour Holiday Park was for sale.'

'That's partly true. But I didn't lie to you. I simply didn't tell you everything. You were a complete stranger, let's not forget. I'm not in the habit of discussing mine or my father's business in the street with total strangers.'

'I told you my business.'

'That was entirely your choice.'

'I see. But you found no reason to reciprocate? When you left me in the car park this morning, I did wonder if I'd ever see you again. But what surprised me most wasn't the way you disappeared so suddenly with what I now realise was a fake illness. No. It was the fact that you'd only spent time with me so that you could suss out your competition.'

'Competition?' Now she was getting annoyed. This wasn't going the way she'd hoped. 'Until you volunteered the information, I had no idea who you were or that you were interested in buying the site yourself. I didn't even know anyone else was interested. The agents didn't mention it.'

'Oh really? You expect me to believe that?'

'It's the truth.'

'Your truth? Or the real truth? Only they seem to be a little different.'

'The real truth.'

'Okay. Assuming I accept that. Once you'd met with the Turners this morning, you knew. Don't look so surprised. They called me this afternoon and told me about your meeting. So then you knew we were in competition. But you still went to Seahorse Bites Café right after that and tried to find out all you could about me.'

'No I didn't. I went for a cup of coffee and to find out if there was any gossip about the sale of the site. A woman called Lilith was the one talking about you.'

'So you didn't ask Josie for my phone number?'

'Er. Yes. I did. But not because of the site. That was because of dinner tonight. Once I discovered you were interested in the holiday park, I did actually think it might be best to cancel.'

'Why? Because you'd found out everything you needed to know about me?'

'No! Look. Could we discuss this inside, please? Over a glass of wine, perhaps.' She held the bottle up again. 'It may be April but it's freezing out here. And I'm not exactly dressed for this weather, as you can see.'

She opened her leather jacket to reveal her low cut, strapless dress and tingles shot up and down her spine as his eyes scanned her body. Without another word he stood to one side to let her in.

'Thanks.'

His gaze travelled the length of her body once again and he bent his head to one side, a questioning look in his blue eyes.

'Why did you come here? We were supposed to meet at the restaurant at 8 but it's only around 7 and you're clearly dressed for an evening out. Are you here to tell me in person you've made other plans?'

'No. I was hoping we could still have dinner. But I didn't want to walk into the restaurant only for you to throw me out. I thought it was safer to come here and see where things stood.'

She gave him a comical sort of smile mixed with a hint of nervous apology and was rewarded with a brief twitch of the corner of his mouth.

'I wouldn't have thrown you out.' The twitch turned into a small grin. 'I have staff to do that if needs be.'

'Good to know.'

'If you're staying for a while I suppose I should offer to take your jacket, and open that bottle of wine. Are you staying?'

'I'd like to. Yes. Does this mean I'm forgiven?'

She handed him the box and the wine while she shrugged off her jacket. He slid the bottle under his arm, and looped the ribbon on the box over his little finger, leaving his other hand free to take her jacket which he hung in a hidden cupboard in the panelled wall of the hall.

'Possibly,' he said, his eyes filled with admiration. 'You look beautiful.'

'Thanks. You look pretty good too. Especially now you're not caked in mud.'

He grinned, and that turned into a smile but his eyes held a curious look and he furrowed his brows.

'If I didn't know better, I might think that you knew who I was this morning and that you tried to do away with your competition.' The smile still hovered around his mouth even though he was trying not to show it.

'I wouldn't have swerved to avoid you if

that were the case.'

'Good point. Unless that's just what you want me to think. Perhaps you've got some other devious plot to get rid of me and that's why you've come here and not to the restaurant.'

She laughed out loud. 'I think someone's been watching too many crime shows on TV. I don't have a devious plot to get rid of you. Besides. I don't need to.'

'Oh really? Come through.'

He led the way into a sumptuous sitting room where a log fire crackled in a massive hearth with a black marble surround and mantle. Two large sofas sat either side of the fireplace, one, a midnight velvet, the other a similar coloured leather. The polished oak floor had one large rug and a couple of ornate, oak tables between the sofas and the fire. A crystal chandelier hung from the ceiling rose and three crystal lamps were spaced around the room on small side tables.

It wasn't at all what she expected. She had imagined a more contemporary décor.

'This is very cosy, especially for such a large room.'

'Thanks. Sit wherever you like. I'll get some glasses.'

She walked across the room and studied several photos in silver frames. They were all of family and friends, she assumed. He was

in a couple with an older man who looked
rather distinguished. That was probably his
dad who was still in Hell. But Mikkel had said
he would be coming to visit soon and she had
a sudden urge to meet him. Which was
ridiculous.

She took a seat on the velvet sofa and
sunk into the cushions just as Mikkel
returned with the glasses. He opened the
wine and poured, handing one glass to her
before sitting on the sofa opposite.

She raised her hand to her brows and
pretended to search for him.

'Oh there you are,' she joked. 'You're so
far away.'

'There's safety in distance.' He raised his
glass. 'Cheers.'

'Cheers.' She raised hers before taking a
sip. 'Safety? You don't still think I'm here to
bump you off, do you?' She laughed.

He eyed her over the rim of his glass, a
strangely sexy smile hovering on his mouth.

'To be honest, I'm not entirely sure why
you're here.'

'Oh. Would you rather I weren't?'

'I didn't say that.'

'But you're uncomfortable with me being
here. Why?'

He raised his brows. 'Didn't we just
establish that we're competitors? And that
you withheld the truth from me earlier. This

morning I thought I was asking a beautiful woman who was here on holiday, to have dinner with me tonight. Now I'm not sure what to think.'

'I'm here because an extremely attractive man asked me to dinner. And because I want a look around his house.'

'Is that what you want? A look around my house? Do you think that might give you more information about me which you can then use to your advantage in your quest to purchase the holiday park?'

'The holiday park has nothing to do with the reason I'm here. But I would like to get to know you better.'

'Why?'

'For personal reasons.'

'Personal reasons?'

'Yes. Because I like you. And because, all day, I've been looking forward to seeing you again. And that's a first for me.'

He looked pleased about that.

'I was looking forward to seeing you too. Even after I discovered who you were.'

She smiled her sexiest smile.

'So do I get to take a look around?'

'My home?'

'Yes. And in particular, your bedroom. I've been thinking about that all day as well.'

He gave a sort of strangled cough, blinked twice and made a valiant effort to compose himself.

'Not all day, surely? Weren't you thinking of how to get your hands on Seahorse Harbour Holiday Park for a great deal of it?'

She ran her forefinger around the rim of her glass and licked her lips.

'I was. That's true. I've spent half the day thinking about that. And the other half about how to get my hands on you.'

Now he choked and spilt several drops of wine down his shirt.

'Sorry,' she continued. 'I thought you wanted me to tell the truth.'

He pulled a handkerchief from his trouser pocket and dabbed at his shirt.

'Is that what you're doing? Are you sure you're not trying to throw me off balance?'

His eyes met hers and locked.

'Could I throw you off balance, Mikkel? Tell me. What have you been thinking about today? And remember. We're supposed to be telling the truth.'

He took a gulp of wine and topped up his glass, holding the bottle out towards her but she shook her head as slowly and as seductively as she could.

'I think you know the answer to that question.'

She leant forward and balanced her elbows on her knees, toying with her wine glass between both hands.

'Do I?'

'Yes. I think you do.'

'Seahorse Harbour Holiday Park and your eco hotel?'

He shook his head as a devilish grin appeared.

'Surprisingly not. At least, not until I got a certain call this afternoon. Then, I'll admit, it did occupy my thoughts.'

'And now? What are you thinking about at this precise moment?'

'I'm thinking I'd very much like to show you my bedroom. But I'm also thinking that could be a big mistake.'

'Because...?'

'Because we both want Seahorse Harbour Holiday Park. And only one of us will get it.'

'But that's business. Don't you switch off from that in the evening? Tonight was supposed to be about pleasure, I'd assumed. That was why you asked me to have dinner with you, wasn't it?'

'Before I knew who you were. Yes.'

'Who I am doesn't make any difference.'

'It does to me.'

'Why?'

'Because you told me that business was a pleasure. I'm not sure where that leaves me.'

'I did. That's true. But surely we can both

put business aside, can't we? Even if it's only for one night. We're also just a man and a woman who are attracted to one another. Deeply attracted, in my case.'

'Ditto. But I was hoping for more than one night when I met you this morning.'

'Were you? Now who isn't telling the truth? You thought I was here on holiday. That's hardly conducive to a long-term relationship is it? Besides. We might not get on.'

'I hadn't thought it through at the time. I had just almost been killed. And I think we will get on. I think we'll get on like a house on fire. And that's also a problem.'

'Perhaps. But I think that when two people meet and feel an instant attraction, and then decide to act on it, they should see that through. The only thing that's changed is that we both want something that, as you rightly say, only one of us can have. But we also both want one another, don't we? Or am I the only one feeling really horny here? Because I am, you know. Desperately. And if you feel the same then I think ... Oh!'

Mikkel had emptied his glass while she spoke, tossed it to one side, strode to the sofa and pulled her passionately into his arms.

'I think it's time you saw my bedroom.'

His desire for her was clear both from the sparkle in his eyes and the gravelly urgency in his voice. She smiled as he pulled her closer.

'You took the words right out of my mouth.'

His kiss confirmed he wanted her as much as she wanted him.

Fourteen

Mikkel opened his eyes long before the sun crept in through the chinks between the blinds and his bedroom windows. He half expected to find himself alone, and to discover that last night had all simply been a dream, but he heard Portia's soft breathing and the scent of her perfume hung in the air, clinging to the sheets.

'Good morning,' he said, as her eyes flickered open and she met his gaze.

Her smile made him want her yet again – and they'd already made love at least three times last night. He couldn't believe how his body and his mind reacted to her. Mind you, just thinking about her most of yesterday had caused sensations throughout his body that he'd never experienced before.

Not even with Diana.

Diana. Oh God!

A sudden wave of guilt swept over him.

But he had nothing to feel guilty about.

'Good morning to you,' Portia said, running her hand slowly down his chest all the way to his stomach and making tiny concentric circles around his tummy button before continuing even more slowly downwards as she eased her body closer.

Diana was quickly forgotten.

He laughed as her fingers tickled, and gasped as he became aroused, and when she slid on top of him and eased herself onto his erection, he moaned her name and gripped her hips with both hands.

He'd always enjoyed sex – he was a red-blooded male, after all – but one-night stands were a rarity for him. He preferred to be in a relationship.

Diana had taken him out of his comfort zone. Affairs with married women were definitely not something he'd ever considered. Until he'd met her. But he'd sort of drifted into that.

He'd felt something for her the moment they met but although he found her extremely attractive, he'd told himself she was off limits.

Then he'd seen how unhappy she was and she'd told him of her husband's constant infidelity. He'd comforted her as a friend, and somehow that friendship turned into something more.

Diana had been the one to start it. And

she'd been the one to end it. Both times.

He couldn't say when exactly, he'd fallen in love with Diana, but it was probably the minute he saw her. And, because of that, and the fact that he was breaking all his self-imposed 'dating' rules for her, he believed she was 'The One'. The woman he might be meant to spend the rest of his life with, or more likely it seemed, have his love unrequited for the rest of his life. Even when she'd called yesterday and he'd done everything in his power to resist her, he had been fairly sure that he would fall under her spell once again.

And then a beautiful blonde – or more aptly, another beautiful blonde, had almost run him down. And when he'd looked into *her* eyes he'd felt something he'd only ever felt once before. That his heart had been snatched from his chest and claimed by someone else. Someone who might keep hold of it forever. This time.

He wasn't sure if that was a good thing or not. But Portia had said she was single, so that was an improvement on Diana.

And then he'd discovered that Portia had lied to him. Or withheld the truth at the very least, which had made him so cross he wanted to yell at someone. Anyone.

When she'd turned up on his doorstep he had been astonished. But he'd also been overjoyed to see her again. In spite of what she had done.

The moment she had stepped inside his home, he knew he wanted her to stay. For an hour, or a few, or preferably the night, and ideally, several nights to come.

He knew sex between them would be good. Really good. But what he hadn't expected was that it would be mind-blowingly fantastic. The best sex he'd ever had in his entire life. Neither had he anticipated how much he'd want her. Or how often. He couldn't get enough of her. He was like a parched man quenching his thirst and yet just minutes after he'd been satiated, he thirsted for her again.

Amazingly, it seemed she felt the same need for him.

They might be competitors in business, but in bed, they were definitely equals.

He had no idea what might happen between them in the future.

He wasn't even sure he was really over Diana yet.

But one thing he was absolutely certain of was that while Portia was here in his bed, he intended to make the most of every single second.

Fifteen

Portia hadn't intended to spend the night in Mikkel's bed.

She hadn't even been certain she'd have sex with him – although she had known it was a distinct possibility, especially as she couldn't seem to get thoughts of him out of her head for more than ten minutes throughout the day.

All she had definitely intended to do with him was flirt, and maybe, share a kiss or two and perhaps allow her hands to wander a little, and his hands too. But as for ending up spending the night in his bed, having full-blown sex time and time again – that was something she hadn't expected.

And as for wanting him and needing him and the moment she'd orgasmed, yearning for him to do it again and again and again. That was a surprise.

She liked sex but it wasn't something she craved, or even needed desperately. Yet from the minute she'd met Mikkel's eyes as he had lain sprawled on that grass verge, she hadn't been able to think about very much else but what it would be like to have sex with him.

And once she had, she found herself wondering how it would feel to *not* be able to have sex with him again.

So she made the most of the situation. And, although he'd satisfied her every need, her every whim and her every desire, within minutes of experiencing that euphoria, she wanted to experience it all over again. She needed to experience it. She yearned for it. She yearned for him.

And when he fell asleep, she longed for him to wake up so that she could kiss him and be kissed by him, caress him and be caressed by him, make love to him and be made love to again and again and again.

The problem was, she had never felt this way about any man before. She'd had a couple of relationships, one of which had even lasted for a few years, but she had never felt such intimacy. Not just physically but mentally and – God forbid ... spiritually.

She'd heard people talk about finding their other half, or their soulmate, but she had always thought it was just a saying. Merely a way of expressing how much someone loved another person. She had no idea that it could possibly be true.

She knew how much her dad had loved her mum and how bereft he was when her mum had died, but she didn't fully comprehend how he felt when he said it was as if he had lost half of his limbs. As if he were no longer a complete person. She assumed he'd eventually feel whole again, like she had. She still missed her mum dreadfully; still thought of her constantly, but her dad had told her that sometimes, when he thought about her mum, he felt as if he couldn't breathe, and that was something she'd never understood.

Until now.

As ridiculous as it was – and it really, really was ridiculous because she'd only known Mikkel for one day – she finally understood what people meant when they said they'd found 'The One'. The only person who could touch their very soul. Their being. Who seemed able to permeate their body, mind, bloodstream, every cell and every fibre until it seemed as if two people had merged into one and neither would ever be quite the same again if that bond – that spell, that magic was broken.

This feeling was unbelievable. It was amazing. It was mesmerizingly magnificent.

It was impossible, wasn't it?

It was madness. It was wildly improbable. It was inconvenient.

It couldn't be happening, could it?

It mustn't. It couldn't. It wouldn't.

'I think I'd better go.'

Portia moved out of Mikkel's embrace and sat on the edge of the bed. She felt dizzy and wasn't sure her legs would hold her.

That must be because she hadn't eaten much since lunch yesterday. Hunger would cause this lightheaded feeling.

Except it couldn't be that because Mikkel had briefly gone downstairs at one point in the night and brought back a bottle of wine and a platter of fruit, cheese and biscuits and other nibbles and they'd sat in bed, eating and drinking, talking and laughing.

They'd even discussed their competing bids for the Seahorse Harbour Holiday Park site.

He'd sketched out an image in her head using just descriptions, of what his eco hotel might be like and she'd done the same for her Trulove Hotel. They'd promised one another that each could see the other's plans, when they finally got out of bed. Which neither of them seemed in a rush to do.

Mikkel looked her in the eye. 'I hope, no matter which one of us gets the site, the other won't feel any resentment.'

'I hope you won't feel bad when I get it,' Portia said.

He grinned. 'I hope you'll be happy for

me when I get it.'

'I'm afraid you need to prepare for the fact that you won't get it.'

'And I'm afraid you're the one who needs to do that. I live in the village and I've known the Turners for a while. You're a stranger, and some of the locals are wary of strangers. I know that from personal experience.'

'I won't be a stranger for long. And I have a knack for dealing with people and getting them on my side.'

He grinned. 'That I do believe. But I have connections to the locals and most of them are already on my side. Besides, Trulove Hotels are all built the same, I understand. My hotel will be better for Seahorse Harbour both ecologically and ethically. Not to mention that it'll be more aesthetically pleasing. I'm sure the Turners will pick me.'

'Don't flatter yourself. The deal's as good as sealed. There'll be a Trulove Hotel on the Seahorse Harbour Holiday Park site by next year. And there won't be a composting toilet or a rainwater shower in sight.'

'Just blocked toilets and tepid showers if a concrete Trulove Hotel is built.'

'You wait until you see my plans.' Portia stuck out her chin and gave him a look of superiority.

'You wait until you see mine.' Mikkel laughed and winked at her. 'In the meantime,

I've got a few other plans, but they have nothing whatsoever to do with hotels, Seahorse Harbour Holiday Park, or anything else concerning business.'

He moved the trays to the floor and gently pushed her back onto the bed.

'I've got a few new ideas of my own,' Portia replied, laughing as excitement and longing swept through her yet again.

'It's only around 6 a.m. or just after,' Mikkel said now. 'Do you have to leave so early? I was hoping we could spend more time together.'

'I must, I'm afraid. Things to do, calls to make. That kind of stuff.'

She didn't look at him. If she did, she knew she would probably stay.

'At this time in the morning?'

'I'm an early riser. Up with the lark, as my dad always says.'

'Speaking of early risers and up with the larks.'

The seductive teasing tone made her look round and Mikkel grinned as he lifted the covers.

'Again? Aren't you ever satisfied?'

'It seems not. At least not with you. I can't seem to get enough of you, Portia Trulove. And I must admit, I find that both exciting and a little worrying.'

She laughed and although part of her

was yelling at her to go, another part of her was begging with her to stay.

The begging won out and she lay back down as Mikkel inched towards her and eased himself on top. He gazed into her eyes and kissed her nose, her cheeks and finally her mouth as she wrapped her arms around him and pulled him even closer.

'I find it exciting and a little worrying too,' she said, between their increasingly passionate kisses.

But as he surged into her once more, all she could think about was how each time was better than the last and that, as crazy as it was, this man stirred far more than just her body. This man touched something deep, deep inside her. Something that no man had ever reached before.

And that was more than a little worrying.

That was terrifying.

She couldn't fall in love with Mikkel Meloy. She simply couldn't.

His heart was set on buying Seahorse Harbour Holiday Park. And so was hers. Only one of them could get it.

To lose it might break his heart.

And she had an awful feeling of foreboding about that.

Was she – as ruthless and as business-minded as she was – prepared to do that?

Sixteen

Why couldn't she simply say, 'No' to this man?

'Spend the day with me,' he'd said, after they'd made love in the shower.

Her brain said, 'Sorry. I can't. I've got too much work to do. I've got to tweak the plans for the hotel a little to incorporate a couple of touches that will bowl the Turners over, and make them want a Trulove Hotel on the Seahorse Harbour Holiday Park. Little touches that will blow any idea of an eco hotel out of the water.'

Her mouth said, 'I'd love to. It's Good Friday. One day off wouldn't hurt. And I didn't get to see much of the village yesterday.'

'I'll show you everything Seahorse Harbour has to offer,' he'd said, kissing her again. 'But first, I'll make us some breakfast. Then I'll drive you to Easterhill so that you can get changed.' He'd given her a devilish smile. 'The dress you wore last night was pretty impressive but I assume you'd rather walk around the village in something a little more casual.'

She'd taken a cab to Mikkel's because she knew she'd have a glass or two of wine and she didn't drink and drive. She'd planned to get a cab back a few hours later, not stay the entire night.

She smiled seductively. 'Perhaps I could throw on something of yours.'

He'd laughed at that. 'You could. And I bet you'd look incredibly sexy in anything you selected, but I think, as I'm about eight inches taller than you, you'd be constantly rolling up the trousers. Not to mention having to keep them up with a belt.' He slid his hands onto her waist. 'Your waist is tiny compared to mine. You've got an incredible body, Portia Trulove.' He pulled her to him and kissed her again.

After which – and a good twenty minutes later – they'd needed another shower.

'Perhaps you should take a cold one,' she'd suggested, grinning at him.

She had kept a safe distance between them this time. He'd kiss her again if she hadn't and she knew what would happen after that. They couldn't seem to keep their hands off one another.

'Perhaps you could stop grinning at me so seductively.'

'I'm not grinning seductively. I'm just grinning. Perhaps you could stop giving me that smouldering look with your dreamy, blue eyes.'

'You think my eyes are dreamy?' He'd taken a step closer.

She'd taken a step back, still grinning and nodded. 'Incredibly dreamy.'

'Anything else you like about me?' He'd taken another step towards her.

She'd raised her brows. It would be quicker to list the things she didn't like about him. It was a very short list. In fact, right now, it was empty.

'One or two things.'

He cocked an eyebrow and his smile made her heart sing.

'Just one or two? I'd better try to up my game then, hadn't I? I like several things about you. More than several. Almost everything.'

Her cheeks burned. Her entire face and body were on fire. Her tummy danced an Irish jig and her legs seemed to be melting beneath her.

'Almost everything?' She shrugged as nonchalantly as she could manage. 'What's not to like?' She laughed.

'That we're competitors in business and that you want a luxury hotel on the very site where I want an eco hotel. Now if I could bring you around to my way of thinking, and get you to see that my hotel would be better for the village, that would make you absolute perfection in my eyes.'

He was grinning and his tone was light and playful, but beneath that, deep down, he meant it, she could tell. That alone, should've made her think of an excuse and run, not walk, away.

Instead, when he took another step towards her and gently pulled her into his arms, she abandoned herself to his kisses yet again.

It was gone 10 by the time they eventually sat down to breakfast, despite Portia having first got out of bed at 6 and asked to take a shower.

Mikkel made deliciously creamy, scrambled eggs with mushrooms fried in butter, which he presented on perfectly browned toast. He squeezed fresh oranges for juice, and Portia felt aroused just watching him. He brewed coffee from beans he ground himself, and he disappeared for a moment just prior to serving it all up, returning with a red rose which he handed her, along with a smile to die for.

When she was able to find her voice she asked, 'Is breakfast always like this in your house? Or is this morning special?'

'This morning is special.' He gave her a look that said it was more than that. 'Very special. But it doesn't need to be. I could get used to this very easily.'

So could she.

And that was a problem.

'I ... I'm not good at this sort of thing.'

Her eyelashes fluttered like a butterfly's wings but she couldn't seem to stop them. Her heart was pounding, her mind was racing, her throat felt dry.

This was all too much.

Too soon.

Bad timing.

Nothing could come of this.

'You were pretty good last night. No. You were sensational. And this morning? Well. Words can't express how good you were this morning.' He smiled and took her fingers in his.

'I'm not talking about sex. Sex is easy. I ... I'm talking about *this*.' She waved her free hand in the air at nothing in particular. 'And this.' She gently stroked the rose. 'Romance. I'm ... not good at romance. I'm not looking for a relationship, Mikkel.'

She held his gaze and saw something flicker across his eyes.

'What are you looking for?'

There was a catch in his voice but he maintained a smile.

She shook her head. 'I'm not looking for anything.' Why did that suddenly make her feel sad? She took a deep breath and forced a smile. 'Apart from a site on which to build another superlative Trulove Hotel.'

His smile now looked as forced as hers.

'Only one of us can get that site, Portia. It means a lot to me. I live in this village and I love it here. You can build a Trulove Hotel anywhere. Do you really need to build one here?'

She nodded slowly. 'Yes. This place has special memories for my dad. In fact, it's where he and Mum first met.'

'Oh.' That clearly surprised him. 'I didn't know.' He looked concerned. Conflicted. Troubled. 'That does shine a different light on the matter.' He looked her in the eye. 'So you're determined then?'

She nodded. 'Yes.'

'And there's nothing I can say or do that'll make you change your mind?'

She shook her head. 'No. Sorry.'

'I see.'

The mood had changed. She'd finally managed to say the word, 'No,' to him. But looking at the expression on his face made her feel as if her heart had sprung a leak and her life blood was dripping out of it.

'I think I'd better go.' Her voice was just an octave above a whisper. 'I'll call a cab.'

'No.' He snapped out of it. 'I'll drive you. We ... we're spending the day together, aren't we?'

'I don't know, Mikkel. Is that really wise? I like you. Obviously, I'm incredibly attracted to you. I think we both know that.' She gave a small laugh. 'And spending the day together is a lovely idea. But is it the sensible thing to do? We're business rivals. We both have our hearts set on getting Seahorse Harbour Holiday Park. A friendship between us might cause ... complications.' She lifted her shoulders in a questioning way. 'Don't you think?'

'A friendship? Is that what we're calling what happened between us last night and this morning?'

His eyes narrowed a fraction and a guarded shadow crept over them as his brows furrowed and his jaw tightened visibly.

She shrugged again. 'It sounds better than a one-night stand, doesn't it?'

'A one-night stand? So that's what it was as far as you're concerned? A hook-up? Just sex?'

'Mikkel, we live miles apart. We're

practically strangers. We only met yesterday. What else was it supposed to be? I told you. I'm not good at this. At relationships. At romance. I'm sorry if you expected more. I don't have more to give. My work is my life. My love. Nothing – and no one, has ever come before that.'

'I thought you said ... I thought we ... I hoped...' His voice trailed off and now he was the one to shrug. 'Okay. I get it. I understand. You want the Seahorse Harbour Holiday Park site and nothing, and no one, matters to you more than getting that.'

She nodded. 'Yes. And you feel the same, don't you?'

He met her eyes and quickly looked away. 'I don't know how I feel anymore. But yes. I think I've already expressed how much that site means to me.'

'I do like you, Mikkel. I really do.'

She reached out her hand and the muscles in his forearm tensed beneath her touch.

'Yeah. I ... like you too. But perhaps you're right. Perhaps spending the day together isn't such a good idea. I'll still drive you back to the hotel though.'

'No, please. I ... I think it's best if I get a cab.' She put on a brave smile as she stood up. 'I also think the sooner I do that, the better. Or we may very well end up naked again, if the last twenty or so hours are anything to go by.'

He darted a look at her, the sadness etched on his face quickly replaced with a smile, albeit not as easy, sexy or warm as his smiles had been.

'You're probably right. We do seem to have a problem keeping our hands off each other.' He got up and stuffed his hands in the pockets of his jeans. 'I'll try to keep mine safely tucked away.' But his eyes were already taking on a smouldering look.

'And I'll call a cab and wait for it at the end of your dive. A safe distance away.'

She tried to laugh but it sounded as forced as it was.

'You don't need to do that.' He seemed hurt now. 'You can wait in here.'

She shook her head. 'I think I do. A bit of distance between us would be good right now. We both ... need a bit of space.'

'Do we? Is that what we need, Portia?' He moved towards her. 'Only right now, what I think I need is to kiss you again.'

She sucked in a breath and hurried a few paces towards the door, grabbing her handbag from the floor where she'd left it last night and picking up her shoes.

'Which is why I definitely need to wait outside. Please, Mikkel.' She was virtually begging him to stay away. 'Please. Last night.

And this morning, were wonderful. We'll always have that.'

He frowned. 'That almost sounds like we won't be seeing one another again.'

'We shouldn't.'

'Is that ... is that really what you want?'

She sighed aloud. 'Oh God, Mikkel. Since meeting you yesterday I have no idea what I want. No! Stay there. Please don't come any closer. I ... I need to think. We both do. We mustn't confuse great sex with ... with anything else. Physical attraction isn't anything other than chemistry. That's all this is. Was. Oh, I don't know. I'm going. Thank you for ... everything. I had a really good time.'

'A really good time? Yeah.' He ran a hand through his hair. 'That's what I'm here for.'

There was a strange bitterness in that comment. As if it held some deeper meaning. Some hidden heartache. She didn't dare to ask, even though her heart wanted her to.

'Bye then. I'll see you around, perhaps.'

He stared at her but she forced herself to turn away, taking out her phone and calling a cab as she trudged towards the front door. When she opened it, she heard him call her name – almost like a wolf crying out in the wilderness, and she ran, barefoot, as fast as she could down the drive.

Luckily for her, the cab arrived as she

reached the end of the drive and she dived onto the back seat and slammed the door.

'Easterhill Hotel and Spa, please. And I'm in a bit of a hurry so can we leave right now?'

She saw Mikkel, also barefoot, coming after her, but thankfully the cab driver took her at her word and she fell back against the seat as he sped away towards Easterhill.

Seventeen

'You're not running off with Mikkel's silver, are you?' The cab driver glanced over his shoulder and shot her a look halfway between amusement and concern. 'Only Mik's my mate and I'd hate to be an accomplice.'

'No! Of course not.'

She laughed even though she wanted to cry – which was utterly ridiculous. What did she have to cry about? She'd just had the best sex of her life, and she'd been the one to walk away. Or run. She should be feeling elated. Satisfied. Ready to do battle for the Seahorse Harbour Holiday Park site.

'Then why is Mik standing in the middle of the road looking like he's just lost his shirt? Which he must've done, 'cos he's not wearing one.' He peeked at her via the rear-view mirror. 'Or is that none of my business?'

She tried not to turn and look but it was a losing battle. The cab driver was right.

Mikkel did look forlorn, despite the distance the driver had already put between them.

'Let's just say, it's personal.' She gave him a quick smile. 'But if he's your friend, I can see why you might be concerned. Especially as he's in the middle of the road. Which he seems to do a lot.' She shook her head and sighed. 'We … er … had a bit of a difference of opinion. Nothing earth shattering. But I think, perhaps, Mikkel had something else he wanted to say.'

'And you didn't want to hear it?'

'No. I didn't.'

The driver let out a loud sigh and tutted.

'The poor guy doesn't have much luck with women these days. First Diana and now you. I'm Jonno, by the way. I hope you haven't broken his heart again.'

'Again? Oh! Er … No. Did you say Diana? Not Josie's sister, Diana, surely?'

'The one and only. D'you know her? Diana, I mean. You obviously know Josie. She's great, isn't she? Josie, that is. Diana's … well, Diana.' He grinned via the mirror.

'I don't really know Josie or Diana. I met them both yesterday in Seahorse Bites Café. But … are you saying that Diana broke Mikkel's heart?'

'Twice.' He gave her a serious look, again via the mirror. 'But you didn't hear that from me. I shouldn't even be telling you that.

You're the enemy, aren't you?'

'Enemy? Oh. You've heard about Seahorse Harbour Holiday Park, haven't you? But how do you know who I am?'

He smiled. 'Seahorse Harbour's no metropolis. It's not even a quarter of the size of Easterhill. Word travels fast around here. Besides, I live in the village and I know all the locals. And you're not local.'

'I'm Portia. Portia Trulove. But I'm no one's enemy. Or at least I don't want to be.'

'Seahorse Harbour Holiday Park is dear to a lot of people here. The fact the Turners are selling is enough to cause uproar in the village. At least they know Mik, and they know he'll take their opinions and concerns into account if he builds his hotel. No one knows you. Sorry, love but they don't. It's only natural that some people might not consider you a friend. Not me though. I can be friends with anyone. Unless they hurt one of my other friends. Then it's a different story.'

'I'm not planning to hurt anyone. And I can fully understand some of the locals being concerned. But a Trulove Hotel in Seahorse Harbour would bring jobs, more tourists, and more money to the village. Surely everyone wants that?'

'Money isn't everything. Happiness is more important. So is love.'

'Perhaps. To some people. Work is what's important to me. So ... when did Diana break Mikkel's heart? And why twice? She's married, isn't she? I saw wedding, engagement and eternity rings on her wedding finger. Was it before she married?'

He eyed her in the mirror as they waited at a set of traffic lights, the engine ticking over slower than her racing heart.

Was he going to tell her? Why did she even want to know? It shouldn't matter to her if Mikkel had been in love with someone. Or if that woman had broken his heart.

Twice.

He must've loved Diana a lot for it to happen twice.

Perhaps he was still in love with her.

But if so, surely he wouldn't have seemed so keen to be with Portia?

'Someone else will tell you if I don't,' Jonno said. 'I'd rather you hear the truth and not some fabricated version. Yeah. It was Diana Dunn. And it was just last year. She and her husband, Alex had been going through a bad patch. She and Mik were friends and last year, around this time, they had a bit of a fling when she and the kids were here on holiday. Then she went back to her husband. They've got a house here which they only used for holidays at the time. She came back in the summer, and Josie came over from New York. Diana restarted things with Mik and she even separated from Alex for a month or two, but it wasn't long before she took Alex back. He almost died at Christmas so the whole family live here now. Not easy for my mate to cope with, as you can imagine. Mik took it really hard. He deserved better.'

Portia couldn't take it in. Mikkel had be so in love with Diana that he'd effectively been at her beck and call, it seemed. And then the woman had dumped him, twice. And that was only a few months ago.

Now Portia remembered the persistent way Diana had asked questions in the café yesterday. Did Diana still have feelings for Mikkel, in spite of going back with her husband? Or was she one of those women who didn't want anyone else to have him even though she no longer wanted him for herself?

And how did Mikkel feel?

Last night and this morning he'd made Portia feel as if she were the only woman in the world. He'd seemed keen to see her again. He certainly seemed eager to spend the day with her. And to make love with her again and again and again.

Was he doing that to get Diana out of his system? Was he trying to convince himself that Diana didn't matter to him one bit?

Was yesterday and today all some sort of elaborate scheme to forget about the woman he really loved? Did he still love Diana? If Diana decided she wanted Mikkel back, would he go to her?

As if reading her thoughts, Jonno added: 'The problem is, Diana can't seem to make up her mind. One minute it's Alex she wants to be with, the next, it's Mik. What's a guy supposed to do when he's in love with a woman like that?' He met her look and grimaced. 'Sorry. Just realised I might be speaking out of turn here. It doesn't take a genius to guess you spent last night at Mik's, and I doubt it was in a guest room. It's none of my business, I know, but I can tell you my mate is one of the most honest and decent guys you'll ever meet. He doesn't play emotional games with women and he doesn't lead them on.'

Was she really having this conversation with her cab driver? She almost laughed at the absurdity of it. But Jonno was Mikkel's friend so perhaps it wasn't that bizarre. Even though it felt it. She wasn't in the habit of discussing her sex life with her own sister, let alone a cab driver she'd just met.

And what was Jonno implying? That if Mikkel had slept with her, he might be over Diana? Unless Mikkel had actually told Jonno that was the case, the man couldn't

165

possibly know, could he? We all think we know how people will react in certain situations, but often they surprise us.

'That's good to know,' she said, unable to think of anything better to say. 'But what Mikkel does or doesn't do is no concern of mine. And while I'm not usually in the habit of discussing my personal life with people I hardly know, I will say this...' She smiled at him via the mirror. 'I'm not looking for a relationship and I believe your friend understands that because I made it very clear. I'm here on business and that, and only that, is all that matters to me.'

He grinned broadly. 'I seem to recall Josie told me something along those lines the first day she arrived here last summer. That she wasn't looking for a man, or love, or anything like that. Now she's living with one of my other mates, Liam Fulbright.' He chuckled so hard his shoulders looked like a pneumatic drill. 'All I'm saying is that a lot of people seem to find the love of their lives here. And I'm speaking from experience. I met my wife, Sandra when she came to Seahorse Harbour for a holiday.'

A tingling sensation made Portia shiver. 'That won't be happening to me.'

'We'll see.' The grin wavered for a moment. 'I'd appreciate it if you didn't repeat what I told you about Diana.'

'I won't breathe a word to anyone. And I'll be leaving in a couple of days, so it's not going to be an issue, I promise you.'

'Thanks. I hope you have a good stay, but I don't suppose you'll be surprised to hear that I hope it's my mate who gets Seahorse Harbour Holiday Park, even though my better half wouldn't dream of staying at an eco hotel. Sandra's definitely a luxury hotel kind of woman.' He winked and the grin returned.

'I'm not surprised at all, but it's good to know that if it ever came down to a vote, I might get Sandra's support.'

Eighteen

Mikkel trudged back up the drive towards his house, only now realising that his feet were bare and seemed to be finding each and every loose stone, wind-blown thorn and even a dollop of seagull poo.

Which pretty much epitomised his life over the last year.

He had thought he was on the road to an almost perfect life, only to find it was strewn with potholes and hit a bloody great dead end.

Meeting Portia yesterday had given him a ray of hope. Perhaps there was a new path he could take to happiness.

But nope. Just another stop sign, smack bang in the face.

What was it with him and women lately? He'd never had this much trouble before.

But then he'd never been in love until he'd met Diana. Not really in love.

For all the good that had done him.

And just as he was beginning to believe he might be finally starting to get over the heartache Diana had caused, she'd called him up and toyed with his heart and his mind once more. But he'd been firm and held his ground. It was either him or Alex. She had to choose.

And then Portia Trulove had appeared from nowhere and bowled him over.

Well, from Easterhill and had almost run him down, but there was no point in splitting hairs, was there?

The fact was, he'd felt something the moment he'd stopped ranting at her and looked her in the eye. And it had taken his breath away for a moment. No. She had taken his breath away.

He'd only felt something similar once before – when he had met Diana.

Was it simply coincidence that both women were blonde and beautiful?

He would make a mental note. In future, avoid blonde beauties at any cost.

Now he had two women he had to try to forget. Two women he knew could ruin his day, or make it feel as if he were basking in sunshine, depending on what they said or did.

When did he become so pathetic? Because that was exactly how he felt right now. Pathetic. And more than a little despondent.

This wasn't him. This wasn't the type of man he was. He needed to get a grip. The sooner the better.

He also needed to remind himself that if he intended to chase a woman down his drive, it was a good idea to put on a pair of shoes.

Yet another lesson Love had taught him.

Love? Pah! Love could shove itself where the sun doesn't shine. He didn't want anything more to do with it. Love had made a fool of him for the very last time. Not that he was in love with Portia. How could he be? He'd only met her yesterday.

And was he really still in love with Diana? Would he have slept with Portia if he was?

Damn it! Why did he have to go and think about sleeping with Portia? Not that they'd done much sleeping. But now all he wanted was to hold her in his arms again. To feel her soft, golden skin pressing against his; her silken hair brushing against his face; her long, agile legs wrapping slowly around him; her mellifluous voice whispering his name.

'Stop it, man! Stop it right now.'

His raised tones startled a pair of seagulls who were doing a dance on his front lawn, trying to entice the worms beneath to raise their heads so the gulls could chew them to bits. The gulls squawked, flapped their wings and ha-ha-ha'd at him. Just like they had yesterday.

'I'm glad you two find my love life so amusing. It's not so funny from where I'm standing, I assure you.'

And he cursed out loud as the sole of his left foot found the longest, sharpest, stone on the entire length of his drive.

Nineteen

Portia needed to avoid Mikkel as much as possible, which meant she had to stay away from Seahorse Harbour. The village simply wasn't big enough to take a chance that she wouldn't bump into him somewhere. There was only one pub, which Mikkel owned, so she definitely couldn't go there. Ditto, the restaurant. He'd suggested going to Seahorse Bites Café for breakfast yesterday, so she couldn't even risk returning there.

She hadn't been to Fulbright Ceramics. But it would be just her luck that Mikkel decided he wanted to purchase some pottery, so perhaps she'd save her visit there for another day.

Instead, she elected to spend the day in the spa. She enjoyed being pampered and although the treatments on offer at the Easterhill Hotel and Spa weren't as varied – or as expensive, as the ones at a Trulove Hotel, they would ease her troubled mind and soothe away the tension in her body, just as much as a Trulove Hotel spa treatment would.

On the way from her room, her dad called for an update. Not that there was any update to give, so she simply reiterated that she was sure the Turners would lean towards the Truloves.

In reality, she was starting to have doubts as to whether that would be the case, but she didn't want to mention that to her dad. She had never let him down before and she still hoped she could save the day.

Tommy would never tell her he was disappointed, she was well aware of that. He would say she'd done an excellent job, as always but that this time it hadn't worked out. But she would feel that she had failed him, and she couldn't bear the thought of that.

She was pondering what options she had when she entered the pool area for a pre-pampering swim. She heard someone calling her name and after scanning the rows of loungers, was astonished to see Lottie and Elsie, two of the women she'd met at Seahorse Bites Café and again in Easterhill shopping centre yesterday. They were munching on cakes and drinking champagne at a table near the huge window which overlooked the grounds of the hotel.

'Come and join us,' Lottie and Elsie said in unison, both laughing at the fact they'd said exactly the same.

Portia hesitated. She had hoped she would have this time alone to clear her head. On the other hand, Jonno's information was still whirling around in her mind and perhaps these women could shed some more light on Mikkel and Diana's relationship. Elsie had said that Diana was her niece, so it was reasonable to assume that Diana might share some secrets with her aunt.

'My fiancé paid for this as a treat for Mum and me,' Lottie said, even though Portia hadn't asked. 'His parents and his sister, Sorcha are coming to stay with us on Sunday and although I know they like me, I still feel a little nervous at the prospect. There was a bit of drama the last time Sorcha was here and I'm worried I might say the wrong thing. You know how it is.'

Portia had no idea 'how it is', but there was no point in saying so. Instead, she nodded and smiled.

'I thought you'd be marching around the village,' Elsie said, with an amused glint in her eyes, 'taking notes and sizing everything up. Sit by me.' She patted the seat beside her which was opposite Lottie.

Portia sat down. 'Marching isn't something I tend to do.' She maintained her smile. 'And I take notes and size things up before I go on a site visit, so when I do wander around the village, it'll merely be to take in the sights and enjoy the delights of Seahorse Harbour, just like any other tourist.'

'Is that so?' Elsie grinned into her glass as Lottie called over a staff member and requested another glass for Portia. 'I heard that you've been enjoying one sight in particular. Although I try not to listen to gossip.'

'Mum!' Lottie tutted. 'What Portia and Mikkel do is no one else's business. I hope you're okay though, Portia. Lilith said she saw you running down Mikkel's drive this morning, with Mikkel chasing after you. It sounded rather strange, but Lilith has a knack of often being right, so...' Lottie shrugged and gave Portia a questioning look.

This was unbelievable. Were she and Mikkel now the gossip of the village? That was all she needed.

'I'm fine, thanks. I was just in a hurry, that's all.'

She didn't bother to explain. It was none of their business. She did see the irony in that though. After all, she was hoping to extract some information, or basically gossip, about Diana and Mikkel.

'We knew it was nothing as dramatic as

Lilith was implying,' Lottie smiled.

Portia couldn't care less what people thought, yet she asked, 'Oh? What was Lilith implying?'

Elsie patted Portia's leg. 'Sometimes it's best not to know what people like Lilith Shoe say. The sad thing is, she just can't help herself. She doesn't mean any harm but gossip can cause all sorts of trouble.'

'Yes. I expect it caused some trouble for Diana when gossip spread of her affair with Mikkel. It seems I'm not the only one to experience that particular pleasure.'

Lottie's mouth formed a perfect 'o'. Elsie frowned but an odd sort of smile crept across her mouth and, as the extra glass arrived at their table, she poured Portia some champagne and handed the glass of bubbly to her.

'I see you're not the type of woman to be easily fazed. I like that. And you're right. It did cause Diana some problems, but not for long. Like you, I suspect, Diana is a woman who likes to get what she wants. If that involves dealing with a few wagging tongues, then so be it.'

'Sorry. I apologise. I shouldn't have said that. I'm not usually the bitchy type. Thanks for the bubbly.'

Elsie gave her a genuine smile. 'I love Diana dearly but I'll be the first to admit she doesn't always make the wisest choices. Her husband, Alex is a highly respected surgeon and a genuinely nice guy when he wants to be. He does have a seriously bad problem with a wandering eye though and Diana has put up with a good deal of crap throughout her marriage. Mikkel was in the right place at the right time. Or the wrong place, wrong time, depending on one's point of view. In my opinion, he was the best thing that happened to Diana, but she chose Alex. I believe she may be having second thoughts right now. I'm not going to put my foot into this apparent triangle, but I'll give you a word or two of advice if I may, which you can take or leave as you wish. Don't make the same mistake Diana did. Men like Mikkel don't come along very often.'

Portia wasn't completely certain what Elsie was saying but she was somewhat surprised it had been said. Was Elsie really telling her not to let Mikkel get away?

'I agree with Mum,' Lottie mumbled, fiddling with the stem of her glass. 'I wasn't here when what happened between Diana and Mikkel took place and I haven't known either of them, or Alex, long, but Mikkel is honest, decent, hardworking and loyal. Not to mention, handsome. He's the type of man most women dream of. A lot like my fiancé, Asher. Asher has made me happier than I ever thought it was possible to be. One day, some lucky woman will realise that Mikkel could do the same for her.'

Now Portia was really confused. Were these two saying Diana should see that Mikkel was the man she should be with? Or were they both saying that Portia needed to see that he could be the man for her? Or were they merely generalising and talking Mikkel up?

People who lived in Seahorse Harbour were definitely weird.

Twenty

Mikkel could tell Diana was upset before she opened her mouth. Her entire body gave off an aura of pent-up frustration and confusion. Her beautiful face was flushed with anger but her eyes were filled with pain.

'How could you do it, Mikkel?'

She was clearly wound up tighter than a coiled spring as she paced back and forth across the floor of his kitchen.

She'd turned up unannounced shortly after he'd returned home from the lunchtime rush at The Seahorse Inn, and demanded to speak to him. At first he'd been tempted to tell her this wasn't a good time but he could see it wasn't a good time for her either, so he caved.

He didn't need to ask what she was referring to. He'd already heard the latest gossip in his pub. He was disappointed it was about him but not at all surprised. He loved living in Seahorse Harbour but the one thing he didn't like was the perpetual gossip.

It was something he'd had to learn to live with, and in reality, Seahorse Harbour was no different to any other village, or for that matter, that much different from his hometown of Hell. People gossiped there just as much.

The only way to avoid being gossiped about, anywhere on the planet was probably to live like a monk, which was something he would never do. And besides, with people like Lilith Shoe around, even a monk wouldn't be immune.

'I could ask you the same question about Alex. How could you have gone back to him?'

'That's completely different.'

The look of surprise on her face was almost laughable. She clearly believed it was. That her sleeping with her husband was in no way as bad as him sleeping with another woman regardless of the fact that both he, and the woman in question, were single, whereas Diana wasn't.

'It's not, Diana. And it wasn't as if I hadn't told you it might happen.'

'Told me? When?'

He let out a tiny sigh. He really didn't want to be having this conversation.

'Yesterday. I told you I'd met someone and that we were having dinner together. I told you I liked her.'

She stopped in her tracks and glared at him.

'But you didn't say you were going to jump into bed with her the first chance you got. You told me I needed to make up my mind and choose between you and Alex. You didn't say I only had a couple of hours to do that or you'd move on to someone else.'

'This is ridiculous, Diana. I'm sorry, but it is. I haven't moved on to someone else, as you put it. What happened last night has nothing to do with that. But I can't wait around for you. I told you that. I thought I'd made that clear. We both need to get on with our lives. And for me, that means I'll be seeing other women and, I hope, sleeping with them.'

'So now you've turned into Alex. Jumping into bed with every woman you meet.'

'Diana! That's not fair. It's not true, either. I didn't mean women in that sense and you know it. I told you I want a relationship. I want a woman who loves me – and only me. But it seems that isn't as simple as it sounds. I'm not planning on sleeping around, but I will see as many women as I need to until I find that special person I can spend the rest of my life with. It's not just women who want that fairy tale, happy-ever-after ending. Men want it too. I want it. And at this point in my life, I'll do whatever it takes to find it.'

'And if I told you, you could have that with me, you'd stop seeing this bloody Portia Trulove woman?'

He wasn't sure how to respond to that. Was it a hypothetical question? Or had she finally made a choice? They stared at one another in silence for a second or two.

'Are you saying I could have that with you?'

'Yes. I ... I think I've made my decision.'

She didn't sound one hundred per cent certain. Her voice faltered as she spoke, and using the word 'think' wasn't exactly committing herself to her choice.

'You "think" you've made a decision? What does that mean? I told you yesterday, and I thought I'd made it abundantly clear, I can't get on this merry-go-round again. Either you're leaving Alex or you're not. Thinking about it doesn't cut it.'

'Sometimes you can be mean, Mikkel Meloy. Do you know that?'

'Yes. And sometimes, so can you. I'm sorry. But this is getting us nowhere. We're exactly where we were.'

'Not exactly. You've had sex with another woman since then. And talking of being mean, Portia Trulove wears that particular crown. I've looked her up on the internet and she's not as wonderful as you seem to think. Did you know she was engaged not that long ago?'

His heart stopped for a nanosecond. Engaged?

He shook his head and could hardly find the words.

'She told me she was single.'

'Oh, don't worry. She didn't lie to you about that. She is single again now. She broke off her engagement as soon as the ink was dry on the purchase of the group of three hotels her former fiancé owned. Yes, that's right. He owned some hotels she wanted and she got engaged to him to get them. It's all there in black and white. You can read it for yourself. It seems she'll do anything to get what she wants. And this may come as a nasty shock to you, but I suspect what she wants isn't you, Mikkel. It's Seahorse Harbour Holiday Park and sleeping with you is the way she thinks she'll get it.'

Something between a derisive snort and a heartbroken laugh escaped him.

'Then she can't be as clever as she thinks because sleeping with me won't get her the holiday park. I don't own it. The Turners do. As I know you're well aware. And Portia definitely is.'

'Yes. And she is clever, Mikkel. Very clever. You're her only competitor. If you back out, the place is hers and she can probably get it for a bargain.'

'If I back out? Why would I do that?'

'You'd do it for her. And I'm fairly sure she knows that. She's the sort of woman who does a shed load of research. And don't forget, she was asking us about you in Seahorse Bites Café. And I suspect she's asked other people about you, too. She's probably got a file about you. She no doubt knows that you're the sort of man who will do anything for the woman he loves. Anything, Mikkel. Including handing Seahorse Harbour Holiday Park over to her, all neatly tied with a red rose and a ribbon. She's taking you for a ride, Mikkel. In more ways than one. But it seems you're too infatuated with the bloody woman to be able to see it.'

He stared at Diana and something recoiled inside him.

He might still be a little in love with her, or maybe a lot – he wasn't sure precisely how he felt about her at the moment – but one thing he was sure of was that sometimes he didn't like her very much at all.

And one of those times was right now.

Twenty-One

Mikkel couldn't stop himself, but he cursed himself for doing it. The moment Diana had left, or the moment after he'd asked her to leave to be precise, he'd yanked his phone from his pocket and searched the internet for Portia Trulove. This wasn't something he would usually do and it felt a little like stalking but Diana had planted a seed and he had to read the details for himself.

He almost choked when he read the article Diana had referred to. It was high up on the search results so it was clearly a well-read piece. There it was in black and white just as she had said.

"True love? It seems not." The article read: "Does Portia Trulove even know the meaning of those words? If you read my column on a regular basis, you'll know I'm not the biggest Trulove fan. But not even I expected this latest 'dirty trick' from the Ice Queen of the hotel empire. Poor Benjamin

Benenden (what were his parents thinking? Ben Benenden? Really?) has been well and truly played for a prize kipper. Not only has the woman he adored dumped him in the gutter, she's taken the highly respected and exceedingly profitable Benenden Hotel group, and his shirt. Yes, she's got the well-known Benenden logo as part of the deal, along with three of the finest luxury hotels this side of paradise, for an undisclosed figure. And what has poor, deluded Ben got? Apart from a right Royal pasting and a few quid. Absolutely nothing. The woman even had the audacity to keep the ring! It was a rather spectacular diamond solitaire, so that doesn't come as a surprise. Like the sun itself, you couldn't look at it directly or the glare would blind you. And be warned, dear readers, if you look directly at Portia Trulove, you may suffer a similar fate. Just how many hotels does this woman want? To hotel owners everywhere, bolt your doors and close your blinds. Trulove is out to get you, but it's not the kind of True Love you want. Just ask Ben Benenden."

The guy – or girl, was clearly a hack, but was there any truth in the ramblings?

More importantly, was there any truth in the things that Diana had said? That Portia was scheming to get Mikkel to back off from the purchase of the holiday park? That it was the only reason she'd slept with him.

But if so, why had she run off? Surely she would've spent the day with him, wouldn't she? Used the time to get him to like her even more than he already did.

Or was this her plan all along? To get him so confused that all he could think about was her? Because if so, that scheme had worked. All he'd done all day so far was think about Portia Trulove.

And even after reading such a diatribe, he knew he'd be thinking about her for some considerable time.

Twenty-Two

Portia had hardly slept all night. After leaving Elsie and Lottie to have her treatments in the spa, she'd gone back to her room to relax. That hadn't worked. Her mind raced with thoughts of Mikkel.

And of course, of Mikkel with Diana.

Why did that bother her so much? Why did she feel such anguish? Because that's precisely what it was – just thinking about the two of them together.

Was she losing her mind? Is that what was happening?

She needed to talk to someone about this but she couldn't tell her dad. Since losing her mum, he'd been drifting on his own ocean of grief as far as love was concerned. And after six wives, he was definitely no expert on happy ever afters. He'd expected to have that with her mum but life had decided otherwise.

There was one person she could call. Two people, in fact. But was it really appropriate to have such a conversation so early in the morning? At this point, and suffering from sleep deprivation, did she care about such things?

It was just after 7 but she knew they'd both be up. They had a new-born baby to feed.

'Portia?' Ben sounded a little surprised at first. 'Hi. How're you doing?'

'Not so good. Do you two have time for a chat?'

'Angela!' he yelled. 'It's Portia. Pick up the other phone, angel. She wants a chat.'

'Hi Portia,' Angela said a moment later. 'Is everything okay?'

'Not really. Sorry to call you so early on a Saturday but I didn't know who else to turn to.'

'Don't be silly.' Angela's voice was reassuring. Comforting as it had always been whenever Portia had got herself worked up over some issue or other. 'You know you can call us at any time, night or day. That's what friends are for.'

'Yeah,' Ben agreed. 'So what's up? You know we'll help if we can.'

'I love you two, you know that, right?'

'We know,' they said, their smiles evident in their tones.

'Okay. This is going to sound really weird. Especially coming from me and particularly bearing in mind what happened with us. But I'm not sure what's happening to me and I need your input and advice.'

'We're listening,' Ben said.

'Fire away,' said Angela. 'Little Portia's sound asleep so we're all yours.'

'Oh God! What am I like? I didn't even ask how she is. Sorry. Is my gorgeous, goddaughter okay?'

Angela laughed. 'She's perfect. And she loves the bunny you sent her for Easter. She won't let it out of her tiny fingers. They only fit around one of its paws. Do bunnies have paws? It doesn't matter. It's so cute. I'll send you a photo.'

'Oh please do. I'd love to see that. And yes. Bunnies have paws. But I don't think they have paw pads, just furry feet.'

Ben chuckled. 'Trust you to know that. So how can we help?'

'You know I told you both about the village of Seahorse Harbour and the holiday park that's for sale?'

'The place on which your dad's willing to spend a small fortune?' Angela queried.

'Yes. Well, I'm there. Actually, that's not true. I'm in a town nearby. But that's semantics. I've met someone. Someone who lives in the village. And I've never felt about anyone what I felt for him the moment I met him. Sorry Ben. But we all know I'm not good at this stuff.'

Ben laughed. 'We do, but that's great news. Isn't it?'

'Portia!' Angela shrieked. 'You've finally fallen in love. I'm so happy for you. Oh wait. You called because there's a problem. What's wrong? Please don't tell us he's married.'

'He's not. He's single. Although there is a woman, who also lives in the village that he's been having an affair with. She's the one who's married. I'm not sure how he feels about her. But that's not the problem. Well, it could be a problem. I don't know. It's just not the problem I'm calling about. The problem is this: He also wants to buy the site I've come to purchase. And it's his dream to build an eco hotel.'

'An eco hotel?' Angela sighed. 'Dear God. That *is* a problem.'

'Why?' Ben asked. 'What's so bad about an eco hotel?'

Angela and Portia both tutted.

'A lot,' Portia said. 'But you're missing the point. He wants to buy the site and so do I. We have completely different plans for it. When we met we both felt this instant attraction. I know he did too because even though I nearly ran him over he asked me to have dinner with him that night.'

'Wait, what?' Angela said. 'You nearly ran him over?'

191

Portia explained how she and Mikkel met and everything that happened after, particularly the morning she had left his house.

'Now I *am* offended,' Ben said, but Portia could tell he was teasing. 'You never went to bed with me on our first night. In fact, if memory serves me, we didn't sleep together until about our tenth date.'

'But you and Angela slept together on your first date, so perhaps I should be offended too.' Portia laughed.

The relationship between the three of them might seem odd to other people but she was so happy that things had worked out the way they had and that she, her ex-fiancé, Ben and her former personal assistant and best friend, Angela, had remained so close.

'Yes. But that doesn't count because Ben and I had known one another for over three years before that.'

That was true. When Ben had told Portia, just a couple of months after their engagement, that he didn't think things were working out between them, one of the examples he had used to prove his point was that he and Angela, who had been Portia's personal assistant for more than ten years, spent more time talking than he and Portia ever had in the three and a half years they'd been dating.

Portia couldn't argue with that. She knew it was true.

Angela even bought Ben's birthday and Christmas presents, although Portia didn't tell him that until after he and she had split up and he'd started dating Angela.

And all three of them knew that Portia had only agreed to the engagement because Ben had said it would make him feel he did matter to her, and that Ben had only proposed because Angela had suggested that it was time he did.

'If I'd been dating someone for over three years and he hadn't proposed, I'd be wondering why not,' Angela had told them both one night when all three of them were drunk at the opening party of a new Trulove Hotel.

Once Portia and Ben had agreed that their relationship had no future, he'd told her she could keep the ring and that they would always remain friends. She'd bought his hotel group for a very good price and done him a massive favour.

She knew that, as the last surviving Benenden, who hated the hotel industry and wanted to be an artist, off-loading the three hotels and being able to reassure all the staff they would still have jobs was a huge relief to Ben.

The only thing he missed, as he told

Portia during one of their phone chats, was talking to her personal assistant. It was Portia who told him there was no reason why he couldn't call Angela up for a chat.

'And why don't you ask her out while you're at it?' Portia said. 'You two are made for one another if you ask me.'

Ben had done so right away and he and Angela had slept together on their first date. Angela had told Portia all about it. Which also might seem odd to some people, but not to Portia. And when Angela discovered she was pregnant two months into the relationship, Ben didn't hesitate to propose. Portia knew he adored Angela and that Angela felt the same about him.

Portia had insisted that it was time he took back the engagement ring he had given her and sell it to open a savings account for their baby. She'd been over the moon when they asked her to be the child's godmother, and lost for words when they discovered the baby was a girl and decided to call her Portia.

'We wouldn't be together if it weren't for you,' they had said.

'And besides, Portia Benenden has a nice ring to it,' Angela had added.

The only fly in the ointment was a certain tabloid columnist who hated Portia with a vengeance. Portia had no idea why. The only reason she could think of was that the woman's now ex-husband had asked Portia out several times. Portia had always said no because she didn't date married men, but the woman seemed to blame Portia for the breakdown of her marriage and vitriolic comments soon began to appear.

'You can take her to court, you know,' Angela had said. She'd told Ben the same thing.

'I think it's best if we just ignore it. The woman is clearly bitter and extremely unhappy. She's lost the man she loved and she blames me for some reason. I can live with that because I know I've done nothing wrong.'

'But other people will read this rubbish,' Angela insisted. 'Doesn't that bother you?'

'Not really. It's just one newspaper and one small column. People will believe what they want to believe. Does it bother Ben? He told me that it didn't, but if it does, then of course I'll take action.'

'No. He says the same as you. That the woman is sad, bitter and hurt and not to fan the flames by adding fuel to the fire. He says she'll eventually realise her mistake. But once someone puts something out there in writing, it's there forever and a day, thanks to the internet. Anyone can read it.'

Portia had laughed at that. 'I think most people have got better things to do than read the rantings of one woman. But if you want Ben and me to do something – if you really feel that strongly, then we will.'

Angela had sighed. 'No. I suppose not. It's not really about me although Ben is now my husband. But if you two can live with it, then so can I.'

That was the last time any of them gave the column another thought.

'Tell me again,' Angela said now. 'Why did you run away? And barefoot, too. That's serious stuff. But surely, when you saw he'd come after you, you considered turning back?'

'I ran because ... because I got scared, I think. And yes, I considered turning back. Twice, I almost asked the cab driver to do just that. But when the guy started telling me about Mikkel and Diana, I had to hear the story.'

'And that's what you're concerned about now?' Ben queried. 'That he might still have feelings for Diana. Or is it more about the fact that you have feelings for him and that those feelings may impact on the Trulove empire?'

'Both, I think. I've never let feelings come before business and I don't know what to do. And if these feelings are real, and the guy does still love someone else, what am I supposed to do about that?'

'You could ask him how he feels,' Ben

said. 'I know you think you're no good at talking about relationships, but that's really your only option. Or you just sit and do nothing and let everything implode around you.'

'You did run down his drive like a bolt of lightning without stopping to put on your shoes,' Angela said. 'That might've given him the impression you wanted to get away. And that might've made him think you had second thoughts about the time you'd spent together and you'd decided you never wanted to see him again.'

'Angela's right,' Ben agreed. 'Look at this from his perspective. Hurtling away from his home after the best sex you've ever had, doesn't give the right impression. The poor guy's probably thinking one night is all he'll ever have with you.'

'So you're saying I should talk to him?'

'Yes,' Angela and Ben said in unison, and laughed.

'Okay. I'll give that some thought. I know you're right. I just need to think of what to say and how to say it.'

'Start with, "Sorry I ran away. I think I may have feelings for you and this is happening so fast." See what he says and take it from there.'

'It sounds so easy when you say it, Angela.'

'It is easy. You just have to trust your feelings and take a risk.'

'Okay. I'll do it. Thanks, you two. Enjoy the rest of the weekend. And give little Portia a big hug and a kiss from me. I'll pop round to see you all when I leave here but I'm not sure when that'll be. I'll give you a call in a day or two.'

Portia smiled as she put her phone back in her handbag.

Angela and Ben were the perfect couple and now the perfect family.

Would she ever have that?

A husband and a baby?

It was not something she ever really thought about. Not even when she'd got engaged to Ben.

But she was definitely thinking about it now.

Twenty-Three

A call from the Turners at 9 a.m. that morning gave Portia something other than Mikkel to think about.

'We're sorry it's taken us a day or two to get back to you, and we realise this is terribly short notice,' Mr Turner said, 'but would you be able to attend a meeting at our office in the holiday park this morning? Around 11 would be perfect, but if that's not convenient, we can rearrange.'

A meeting on a Saturday morning at Seahorse Harbour Holiday Park was not something Portia had expected. Would this be good news, or bad? Or did they simply want to discuss a few more details?

'Of course. No problem. I'd be happy to.'

She changed out of her jeans and T-shirt into a cotton dress with a delicate floral pattern and discarded her leather jacket in favour of a navy-blue linen one that was the perfect balance between business and casual.

It was a Saturday after all and she wanted to give the impression of a relaxed but professional woman. She swept her blonde hair up into her trademark ponytail, slipped on a pair of navy-blue court shoes in place of the trainers she had been wearing and reviewed her appearance in the full-length mirror.

She smiled at her reflection. The pale blue floral dress brought out the colour of her eyes and highlighted her tan. She liked that.

Perhaps she'd pop into The Seahorse Inn for lunch after her meeting. Mikkel might be there and she wouldn't mind seeing what he thought of her outfit.

Not that it mattered.

Or it shouldn't.

She must stop constantly thinking about Mikkel.

She gathered all her papers together, rolled up the plans and slid them back into their storage tube, popped her iPad into its leather case and slung her handbag on her shoulder. A final look around the room ensured she had everything she needed and with a quick, deep breath she turned and headed out to her meeting.

She hated being late for anything and always made sure she allowed herself ample time to get to meetings but she hadn't anticipated there would be so much traffic either in Easterhill itself or on the road to Seahorse Harbour. It was like rush hour in a big city. She'd expected more cars on the road not only because it was the weekend but also because it was a Bank Holiday weekend, but this was something else.

When she eventually parked her car at the Seahorse Harbour Holiday Park, she had just minutes to spare.

In her rush to avoid being tardy, she didn't change into her wellies. Thankfully, the ground had dried out considerably after Wednesday night's storm and there had been no rain on Thursday or yesterday, but she had to skip over a few muddy puddles nevertheless.

She smiled as she did so and made longer and higher leaps each time, giggling to herself like a child. She had a ludicrous urge to jump into one or two of them and might allow herself to do just that on the way back to her car.

Her happy smile faltered when she reached the Turners' office. Mr and Mrs Turner were both standing by the window, looking out, but far worse than that, so was Mikkel Meloy.

She had no idea what they had been looking at, or whether they'd been looking out for her, but now all three were staring at her with differing expressions on their faces.

Mr Turner looked a little bewildered, as if wondering why a grown woman would be behaving in such a childish fashion. His wife looked amused, as if she knew exactly what Portia had been thinking. Mikkel looked ... at first as if he were cross and then as if he would like to join her, but when their eyes met through the glass of the window, the look in his eyes was something far deeper and more meaningful. And she knew exactly what he was thinking because a moment after she'd spotted him standing there looking at her, she'd been thinking it too.

Thoughts of being in Mikkel's arms, kissing, made Portia's cheeks burn, her heart race and her skin tingle. Tiny beads of perspiration popped up over her body. She hoped she'd have a minute to calm herself before entering the office but as she set her foot on the first step, the door flew open and Mikkel stood in the doorway.

The urge to rush into his arms was almost overwhelming and Portia actually gasped. Yes, gasped.

Oh God. What was wrong with her?

This could not be happening.

She threw him a quick smile before hastily averting her eyes but her voice crackled as she spoke.

'This is a surprise.' She cleared her throat as quietly as she could. 'Good morning, Mikkel.'

He seemed equally discomposed and almost as if he were glued to the spot.

'A lovely surprise. You look beautiful ... er ... I mean. Good morning. Oh. Er.' He moved out of the way to let her pass. 'Sorry.'

The subtle aroma of his aftershave pervaded her nostrils as she passed and she momentarily closed her eyes and breathed it in as images of their night together flashed in her mind's eye.

She coughed to pull herself together.

'Good morning, Mr and Mrs Turner. What a lovely day. But goodness, there's a lot of traffic on the roads this morning. I hope I haven't kept you waiting. How are you both today?'

She stretched out her hand to each in turn and smiled.

'We're both well, thank you,' Mr Turner said, beaming at her. 'And you're bang on time, so no.'

'Good heavens no, dear,' Mrs Turner added. 'You look very pretty today. Those colours really suit you. They bring out your beautiful eyes.'

Portia wasn't sure whether to be flattered or annoyed. She would bet her life on the fact that Mrs Turner hadn't told Mikkel that his bright teal T-shirt brought out his eyes. His gorgeous, blue eyes. Even though it did. And it made his hair seem blonder and his tan deeper and...

Portia coughed again. 'Thank you. You're looking lovely today too. And very summery, if I may say so. The parrots on your dress are delightful.' She could've added, 'and huge and garish,' but she didn't, obviously.

Mrs Turner giggled. The woman actually giggled!

'Parrots are one of my passions.'

'Really? Then I know just the place for you. There's a parrot paradise close to one of our hotels in the Caribbean. I'll email you some details and a few photos. You'd love it there.'

'A parrot paradise? Oh my. That sounds like heaven. Wouldn't that be wonderful, darling?'

Mrs Turner looked fit to burst with excitement as she turned to her husband and tugged at the sleeve of his cardigan.

'It certainly would. But we mustn't think about that right now. I'm sure these young people have other things they'd much rather be doing today than listen to us talking about parrots.'

Portia darted a look at Mikkel. She knew precisely what she'd rather be doing right now. And judging by the look on Mikkel's face and the sparkle in his eyes, he was thinking exactly the same thing.

She gave him a tentative but suggestive smile and he returned it with one that told her all she needed to know. The minute they got out of here, they'd be headed somewhere they could be alone ... and naked.

Portia dragged her attention back to the Turners.

'I'm happy to talk about parrots,' she said, beaming, while praying they wouldn't, and hoping this meeting was short so that she could get her hands on Mikkel. 'But I think you asked us here for other reasons.'

'Yes,' said Mr Turner. 'Yes, we did. Let's all sit down. Would you like coffee? Or tea?'

Portia shook her head. 'No thanks. I'm fine.'

'Mikkel? Have you changed your mind? Would you like something now?'

'No thanks. I'm good too.'

They all sat and Mr and Mrs Turner smiled at one another and then at Portia and Mikkel in turn.

Mr Turner linked his fingers and plopped both his hands on the desk, leaning forward as he did so and giving a lengthy cough as if he knew what he was about to say might be unwelcome.

Portia tensed, fidgeted in her chair and cast a quick glance at Mikkel who was gazing at her as if they were the only ones in the room. She wasn't sure whether she was more nervous of what Mr Turner might say, or more excited at the prospect of sex with Mikkel but she wanted this first part to be over so that she could get to the sex bit as soon as possible.

'Since meeting you on Thursday, Portia, and of course, letting Mikkel know that someone else was interested in our holiday park, Daphne and I have talked of little else. Now I hope I'm not speaking out of turn, but I believe you two ... have become acquainted.'

Portia gave a tiny gasp of surprise and shot another look at Mikkel who, after an initial reaction of shock, grinned devilishly for a moment before becoming serious.

'We have,' he said.

Mrs Turner leant forward now, bringing herself level with her husband.

'You probably think it's none of our business, and we wouldn't usually ask such things, but before we heard that you'd ... met ... we had an idea.' She looked embarrassed but quickly skipped over it. 'And we think it's a rather good one. Or at least, a possibility.'

'It's a very good one, I thought,' added Mr Turner. 'And it solves all our problems.'

Mrs Turner nodded. 'We discussed it with our family and they all agreed it would be the perfect solution.'

'So we wanted to see what you thought.'

'But that was before we heard ... well. You know.'

'Regardless of that, we wanted to run it by you and see if there was any way that it could work.' Mr Turner's smile was huge. 'And the fact you're now ... better acquainted might actually be a bonus.'

Portia exchanged confused glances with Mikkel.

'See if what would work?' Mikkel asked.

Mr Turner looked at his wife as if he didn't understand and Mrs Turner shrugged before clearly realising the problem.

'Oh goodness me. Didn't we say?'

'I thought we had,' Mr Turner said, still looking at his wife.

'I'm not sure we did.'

They looked at Portia and Mikkel and smiled.

'We thought it would be lovely if we could sell Seahorse Harbour Holiday Park to you both.' Mr Turner flopped back in his seat as if a great weight had been lifted from his shoulders.

His wife added, 'It would be wonderful if you could buy equal shares and then build both of your hotels as one. Part eco hotel, part luxury hotel.'

Mr Turner sat up again. 'A luxury eco hotel!' He beamed triumphantly.

'They exist, you know,' said Mrs Turner. 'We suddenly remembered our darling son and dear daughter-in-law went to one for their honeymoon. I thought it was an odd idea, to be honest, but when I saw the photos, I was pleasantly surprised.'

'The place looked amazing,' said Mr Turner. 'We've got some photos on this laptop so we can show you.' He turned his laptop around and clicked a key.

Portia and Mikkel stared at one another before each turned to the laptop and watched the slide show in stunned silence.

Portia already knew the residents of Seahorse Harbour were weird. She hadn't realised, until now, that one or two of them must be completely and utterly insane.

Twenty-Four

'A luxury eco hotel,' Mikkel said as he and Portia waved goodbye to the Turners and walked towards Portia's car. 'That could work.'

Portia stopped in her tracks and stared at him.

'You're not seriously considering their suggestion, are you? Because it wouldn't work. It couldn't. The entire idea is madness. We're from totally independent and unrelated companies, and to even suggest to two entirely separate prospective purchasers that they should pool their resources and enter into a joint venture is utter insanity.'

'I accept it might not be as simple as they seem to think it is, but it's not completely impossible, is it?

'Yes! It is. Besides, it's not what our hotels are about.'

'What? You don't believe in conserving the planet and making the most of natural resources?'

'Of course I do. We do. That's not the part I was referring to. A luxury eco hotel is actually quite a nice idea. It'd be different from most of our hotels but not so different. We already use local produce and services wherever we can. We employ local staff. We ensure we use the most energy efficient and up-to-the minute goods and equipment. Even down to our light bulbs. But composting toilets and rainwater showers, we don't have. Although recycling rainwater is something we do. We use it to water the gardens and various other things. Anyway. The part I meant wouldn't work was the bit about us buying equal shares of Seahorse Harbour Holiday Park.'

'You don't like sharing?'

'No. Not in business matters. Actually. Not in personal matters either.'

He couldn't stop the sneer. The things Diana had told him about Portia and the article he'd read, came rushing back to the forefront of his mind.

'You want total control. And you'll do anything you have to do to get it.'

She looked a little surprised.

'We never do joint deals. We never have. And yes. I suppose so. But you make it sound as if that's a bad thing. Wouldn't you do anything you had to in order to get what you want?'

'Honestly? No. I don't think I would. Not if it meant hurting someone, or lying, or cheating. That's not who I am. And I hope I never will be. I definitely wouldn't have sex with someone, and more than once – several times in one night in fact, just to get the upper hand in a business deal.'

'Are you suggesting I would?' Her perfect brows drew tight together. 'Holy crap! You think that's why I had sex with you!'

'Isn't it?'

'Is that really what you believe?'

He shrugged, unsure again now. He wasn't certain he believed it in the first place but Diana and that article were pretty convincing. And Portia had run off. The look of horror on Portia's face implied he might have got the wrong end of the stick.

'I don't know what to believe. I thought you liked me. I thought something had happened between us. Something out of the ordinary. Something special. We have the best sex ever, and then you rush off. Which leaves me wondering what the hell is going on.'

'And you jump to the conclusion that I slept with you to somehow get the upper hand regarding Seahorse Harbour Holiday Park? How would that work, exactly? You don't own it. You don't have any sway in what the Turners do with it. I'm confused, so please enlighten me. How does me spending the night with you, in any way improve my prospects of buying the holiday park?'

'Because you could persuade me to back off. To let you have the site.'

She burst out laughing.

'You have got to be kidding! I could? It's really that simple?'

She shook her head and her ponytail flew back and forth behind her and Mikkel remembered how soft and silky her hair felt entwined around his fingers.

'You could. I think.'

Her lips parted seductively and her eyes twinkled with a mixture of disbelief, hope and excitement.

'Flipping heck. Let's go. We'll take my car.'

'What? Where? I walked here anyway.' He'd missed something, obviously. 'Where are we going?'

He hurried towards the passenger door as she raced to the driver's side having unlocked the car with the remote.

Their eyes met across the roof as they each placed a hand on their respective door handle.

'To your place. That's closer than my hotel. But just to be clear. I didn't sleep with you because I thought it would help me get the site. I slept with you because I wanted to. I wanted you. And more than I've ever wanted anyone, as it happens. But that's irrelevant now. You think I had sex with you to get the upper hand. Well, if that's all it takes, believe me, I'm more than willing to have sex with you again. Delighted, in fact. And you just said that you'd back off from the site if I did, so we're going to go and have sex. And once I've signed the contract for the site, we could maybe have celebratory sex too. And then sex just because we want it. How does that sound to you? Do we have a deal?'

He'd lost focus on what she was saying shortly after she'd said she wanted to have sex with him. And more than she'd ever wanted anyone, so he wasn't completely certain what he'd be agreeing to. But he'd get to have sex with her and right now, that was all that mattered.

'Er. You may need to run all the rest of that by me again, but as to the having sex right now part, that sounds fantastic. I definitely agree to that.'

'Fine. We'll work out all the rest later. Jump in.'

Clumps of turf and bucket loads of gravel shot up in the air as Portia sped off, but she didn't seem to care and Mikkel was far too eager to get to his house to even worry for one second about the speed she was going or that she might run someone over.

All he could think about right now was getting home and he and Portia getting naked.

Twenty-Five

'I suppose we should talk about Seahorse Harbour Holiday Park at some point.' Mikkel kissed the top of Portia's head as she lay in his arms. 'We did say we'd get back to the Turners by the end of the day.'

'You were the one who said that. I told them I'd need to discuss it with my dad and I'd get back to them asap.'

'When are you going to talk to your dad?'

'I'm not.'

He shifted position so that he could see her face.

'Why not? Don't you need to run something like this by him? Or is he happy to let you make such decisions?'

'He's happy to let me make any decisions I feel would be good for us. But I do often discuss things with him first. Partly because I like to and partly because I value his opinion and if I'm having doubts or concerns, it helps to talk to him. Although not always. I recently made a decision that impacted on our business and it might've gone badly wrong. But he backed me all the way and as it happened, it's actually improved things in more ways than I'd imagined.'

'I'm confused. Why did you tell them you needed to discuss it then?'

'To buy myself time.'

'To think about it?'

She shook her head. 'There's nothing to think about.'

'Er. Still confused. Does that mean you've already made a decision?'

'Of course. I told you. We don't do joint deals. I'm hoping they'll realise the absurdity of their suggestion and see sense. Only one of us can buy the site.'

He wriggled down in the bed so that their eyes were level.

'So where does that leave me?'

Her brows furrowed.

'Exactly where you were this morning before we came here.'

He sucked in a breath and flopped over onto his back, staring up at the ceiling.

'And where does that leave us?'

'Us? Er. Exactly where we are now.' She raised herself up on one elbow and trailed a finger down his bare chest. Her smile was sensual and reassuring. 'Although I believe you did say that if I had sex with you you'd back off from the site and let me have it.' Her voice was sexy and seductively persuasive and she eased herself upwards and looked him directly in the eye, her lips just millimetres from his. 'Will you?'

He almost said yes, but his phone rang as his mouth formed the word, and it felt as if he'd been awoken from a trance.

He grabbed his phone and saw it was the icon of a white butterfly – the icon he'd recently attributed to Diana's calls.

Jesus Christ! What now? Was she calling to tell him she'd left Alex? Wouldn't that just be perfect timing? He hit the reject button and switched the ringer to silent. He couldn't deal with Diana right now.

He turned back to Portia, who was grinning like the cat who'd got, not just the cream but also the keys to the dairy.

'Are you serious?' He hadn't meant to sound so abrupt.

She narrowed her eyes for a second before laughing nervously.

'Of course not. It was a joke. You don't think I took that seriously, do you? Only an idiot would give away the chance of owning Seahorse Harbour Holiday Park in exchange for sex. And you're far from being an idiot, Mikkel. I ... I'm a little hurt that you would think that of me.'

'Was your ex-fiancé an idiot?'

'What?' She pushed herself away from him and twisted round to sit upright. 'How did you find out about Ben?'

'Was he something else you were trying to keep a secret?'

She turned her head to look at him and her eyes were filled with hurt and anger.

'No. And I don't know what you mean. Why did you ask if Ben was an idiot? Of course he wasn't. He isn't.'

'But he no longer owns his family's business logo, or their legacy, or the hotel chain, does he? And he no longer has a fiancée either.'

Her mouth formed a tight line.

'And your point is? What are you trying to say, Mikkel? Why don't you just come out and ask me?'

He pushed himself up so that he sat facing her on the bed.

'All right. I will. Is it true?'

'Is what true?'

'That you got engaged so that you could get the Benenden Hotel group? And then you dumped your fiancé but kept the hotels. Oh, and the engagement ring.'

His heart pounded as he waited for her answer but she stared at him in silence.

After what felt like forever but was only a matter of seconds, she got out of bed and walked, naked, to the chair on which she'd thrown her clothes. Or to be precise on which he'd thrown them when he undressed her.

'You're running off again?'

He tried to keep the fear from his voice and couldn't stop the audible sigh of relief when she took her phone from her handbag and came back to the bed. Just watching her walk made him want her again but he fought the urge and his rising passion, with every inch of self-control he could muster.

She partially covered herself, leaving only her perfect breasts bare to tempt his resolve, pressed a button on her phone and stared at him as she held the phone in the space between him and her.

It was on speaker and only rang three times before a man answered, laughing ecstatically.

'Perfect timing, Portia! Your tiny goddaughter has just said, "Daddum". Angela's a little jealous and is trying to convince me I misheard. But I didn't. And Daddum obviously means Dad, right? What else could it mean? I'm putting you on speaker, so be careful how you answer.'

A woman was laughing in the background and it sounded like a baby was chuckling loudly.

'In your dreams,' the woman said. 'Our little angel was saying, "Ad mum" and was obviously trying to say "That's Mum". You're with me on this, aren't you, Portia?'

Mikkel watched the tight line of Portia's mouth curve into a loving smile and the hurt and anger fade from her eyes, which now sparkled with delight.

'She spoke? Aww! I wish I'd been there to hear her first word. But I think what the little bundle of joy was trying to do was to say, "Dad and Mum". Because she loves you both equally. And she's clearly not one to waste time with three words when one word will do. "Daddum" definitely means Dad and Mum.'

'Awww!' the woman squealed with happiness. 'Of course!'

'Brilliant, Portia!' said the man. 'Yes. And you too my darling little girl. You're so clever. Yes, you are. And you're clever too, big Portia. Perfect answer.' He laughed louder. 'Hmm. This could get confusing. Anyway. Sorry. You didn't call to listen to baby talk. Are you calling to let us know when you'll be here?'

She shot a look at Mikkel as if she'd forgotten he was there.

'No. Sorry. I'm going to be a pain, I'm afraid, and ask you to do me a favour. It'll sound strange so bear with me. Oh, and you're on speaker phone because I'm with someone. I hope that's okay.'

'Er. Right. Yeah, fine. But who else is listening?'

'It's the man I told you I'd met. Mikkel. And Mikkel, these two, sorry, three people are Ben, Angela and little Portia.'

'Hi Mikkel,' Ben said.

'Hello Mikkel,' said Angela.

Little Portia said something incomprehensible and gurgled with laughter.

Mikkel couldn't help but smile even though he was surprised and somewhat confused by what was happening.

'Hello, Ben, Angela and Little Portia. It's lovely to … er … meet you by phone.'

'Okay,' Portia said, serious again now. 'You might want to cover the little one's ears for this. Mikkel seems to think that I … er … went home with him to persuade him to walk away from his offer to buy that site I told you about. He seems to believe that I'll use any means possible to get the place. He's obviously, either heard about or read one of the scathing articles about me and you Ben, and how I stole your hotels and logo from you. Oh, and the ring. Let's not forget the ring. So … without putting words in your mouth, would you mind telling him what really happened? Just the bits concerning me. I'm not asking you to divulge anything personal about the two of you.'

'Ben's your ex-fiancé?' Mikkel was

stunned. He hadn't realised this was *that* Ben.

'I am,' Ben said. 'And you're right, Portia. This is a little weird. But sure. I'm happy to do that. Okay, Mikkel. There're two things you need to know here. Portia was never that in love with me. She loved me, and I think I can safely say she still does, as a friend, but I was the one who persuaded her we should go out and I was the one who pestered her to get engaged. All Portia wanted to do was work, and have a good time with someone she cared a lot about.'

Mikkel studied Portia's face but it was a blank canvas right now. She was clearly trying not to show how she felt about this strange situation, but she smiled as Ben continued. Mikkel though, felt more and more ashamed.

'I was also the one who suggested we split up. Portia was a little surprised and was willing to try harder to make me happy but we both knew what she felt for me wasn't enough for a marriage. And I told her that I spent more time talking with her personal assistant than I did her.'

'That was me,' Angela said. 'I was Portia's personal assistant for years. And also one of her best friends. I'm still one of her best friends even though I deserted my post as her assistant after I fell pregnant.'

'Which was after our first date,' Ben said. 'But we're getting ahead of ourselves. Portia and I continued as we were for a while. The Truloves bought my hotels and the logo. I've never had the slightest interest in hotels. Well, not owning them. Staying in them is great. And as part of our deal, Angela and I, and our family, get to stay in any Trulove Hotel we want, anytime, anywhere, for as long as we want. I still think I got the best end of the deal. I got rid of the hotel chain which had been like a rope around my neck, and for a really good price. Plus free holidays for life. And I also got to keep Portia as a friend. A friend I love and admire. A friend I'd trust with my life. And with my wife and child's lives.'

'The fact Ben and I have named our baby, Portia should tell you all you need to know about how we feel about our friend.'

Angela sounded not only defensive of Portia but also a little peeved that Mikkel was doubting Portia's character.

Mikkel reached out his hand but Portia pulled hers farther away and a flicker of hurt reappeared in her eyes.

He silently cursed himself. How could he have misjudged her so badly?

That was obviously what she was asking herself and why she backed away.

'Thank you both for telling me the truth,'

Mikkel said. 'I should've trusted my gut feelings. I'm sorry.'

'There's more,' Ben said. 'When Portia and I eventually agreed to break up, it was she who advised me to ask Angela out. I'd told her I missed the chats Angela and I had when Portia was out or too busy to take my calls. I thought it would be awkward. Angela was still Portia's personal assistant. But, as always, Portia was right. And on this, she did get her own way. She told me Angela and I were perfect for one another, and we are.'

'And when I discovered I was expecting,' Angela added, 'she was just as excited as we were.'

Ben laughed happily. 'I proposed as soon as Angela told me. And that's when Portia insisted on returning the engagement ring I had wanted her to keep.'

'He doesn't need to know that bit,' Portia said, hastily interrupting.

'Yes, he does,' Angela retorted.

'Yep,' Ben agreed. 'Portia said we should sell it and open a savings account for our baby with the money. Which is exactly what we did. Some people write all sorts of crap about Portia, but most of it is precisely that – crap. She ignores it, and so should you.'

'Someone, somewhere will always find evil things to say about a person for their own reasons,' Angela said. 'Those sort of articles and comments and social media posts say more about the person who writes them than they do about the person being attacked. I get so cross when I read one about Portia, or about my husband, but they both prefer to let them go unanswered, and that's their choice.'

'We think it's better to ignore them,' Ben said. 'I don't know what's happening between you two, only that Portia likes you, because she told us she does. So you should do what we all do and ignore that garbage. And you should thank your lucky stars and just be happy that she likes you. And she'll probably hate me for saying this, but she clearly likes you a lot because she's asking us to talk to you.'

'Thanks Ben!' Portia had blushed crimson.

'I'm grateful she did,' Mikkel said, trying to get Portia to look at him by moving closer to her. 'And believe me. I'll be doing more than thanking my lucky stars once this call has ended.'

Ben laughed and Angela tutted, but in an amused way.

'We'll say goodbye then,' Ben said.

'Wait. Portia?'

'Yes, Angela?'

'If you want to bring Mikkel with you when you come to visit, feel free to do so.'

'Yeah. That'd be good,' Ben agreed.

Now Portia finally met Mikkel's eyes.

'Er ... I'm not sure we're at that stage. Or even if he'd want to meet my friends in person.'

Mikkel took her free hand in his and this time she didn't move away.

'I would. Very much so. And speaking for myself. I was at that stage the day we met.'

'We're hanging up now.' Ben laughed again.

'Thanks for this,' Portia said.

'Anytime,' Angela replied. 'Have fun, you two. Hope to see you soon.'

'Bye. And thank you,' Mikkel said, taking the phone from Portia the second she rang off and putting it on the bedside table. 'I've got some serious apologising to do, haven't I?'

'Yes.' Portia's smile was like sunshine on what could've so easily been a very stormy day. 'I think you have. And does this mean I can now make jokes about you giving me Seahorse Harbour Holiday Park without you thinking I'm some evil witch determined to get her own way?'

He nodded as he pulled her close. 'I never thought of you as a witch. Or as evil. Just a woman who likes to get what she wants. But I did believe you might do anything to get it. I apologise for that. You're not ruthless or cold-hearted. I can see that now. You're wonderful and kind. You're loving and clearly supportive of your friends.'

'Er. I'm no saint, either, so please don't think I am. I do like to get what I want. And I will do almost anything to get it. I will admit that. But I draw the line at certain things. I don't lie, cheat, steal or deceive. But I do use promises of treats – like the free holidays Ben and Angela have, and I do try to persuade people to see my point of view. And before we go any further, there's something else you need to know. I've already offered the Turners free holidays, and I've tried to persuade them a Trulove Hotel would be a much better prospect for the village than your eco hotel would be.'

He smiled and ran a finger down her cheek.

'Which is why they called me after your meeting with them and told me that there was someone else interested in the holiday park. Your charm clearly worked.'

'Or not. They want us to share the site. I need to up my game.'

'Or review your business plan and consider an eco hotel.'

'A luxury eco hotel,' she corrected.

'My eco hotel was going to be fairly luxurious. Not up to a Trulove Hotel, I accept, but composting toilets don't have to be gross, and rainwater showers can be heated and filtered rainwater. Heated and filtered with solar and hydro power, of course.'

'Hmm. Okay. That doesn't sound horrendous. But did you say "was"? Have you already accepted it'll be a Trulove Hotel on the site?'

He grinned. 'Not entirely, no. But I think, perhaps, you need to accept that it might not be a Trulove Hotel either. They clearly like the idea of a joint operation even if you don't. And would it really be so bad? I'm not sure it'd work for me, either, but at least I'm willing to discuss it.'

'Discuss it? Okay. We can do that. But I'd have to see your plans.' She grinned. 'The detailed plans. The architect's drawings, not some sketch you drew on the back of a pub coaster.'

'Very amusing.' He was beginning to understand her humour. 'I'll show you mine if you'll show me yours. And we had already agreed that we would show one another what we had.'

She grinned provocatively. 'Are we still talking about hotel plans? Actually, why *are* we talking about hotel plans right now?'

'Why are we talking at all? Actions can say so much more than words.'

'That's what–'

He cut her short with a kiss, eager to

show her, instead of telling her, exactly what he wanted to say.

That he was rapidly falling in love with her and there was nothing he could do to stop it.

And he was rather pleased about that.

Twenty-Six

Portia couldn't stop smiling as she drove back to Easterhill several hours later.

Unless she was very much mistaken, Mikkel Meloy was falling in love with her. No. He was already in love with her.

Which was exactly what she wanted, because she had fallen in love with him the moment their eyes first met. She simply hadn't realised it was love.

Now she knew it without a doubt.

She wouldn't have phoned Ben and Angela and asked them to tell Mikkel the truth if it wasn't love she felt for him.

She couldn't believe she'd gone to such extremes but when she'd seen the look of doubt and pain and anger in his eyes and he'd said those awful things about her, she would've done anything to prove it wasn't true.

And it was clear to her that he didn't want to believe those horrid things about her anyway. He just needed to be sure. Doubts were understandable, especially as she hadn't told him the entire truth when they'd first met.

Normally, if anyone had said those things and accused her of such behaviour, she'd have simply shrugged and walked away. She didn't care what people thought of her – until she had met Mikkel. Now she cared deeply about what he thought of her, which was both frightening but also exciting.

She opened the car window and let the early evening air blow her hair into a wild frenzy, Mikkel having gently loosened it from the ponytail she had, as usual, tied it in that morning. Now the blonde, soft waves cascaded down to her waist, and thick strands danced madly around her face, lifted by the refreshing breeze.

She wanted to sing at the top of her lungs, to shout out and tell the world how she felt, to dance and spin and laugh and scream with joy. She couldn't remember the last time she had felt like this.

Because she had never felt like this.

Clinching deals made her happy. Work made her happy. Her dad and her sister, Bethany made her happy. Being alive made her happy.

But this. Nothing had ever made her feel as happy as this.

Knowing that she'd just left Mikkel's arms so that she could go to her hotel and get showered and changed and that, in about two hours, she'd be back in his arms again, was nothing short of bliss.

He hadn't wanted her to go.

'You look perfect as you are,' he'd said.

'I'm not going to Hippocampus for dinner stark naked!'

He'd grinned at her. 'Pity. But I didn't mean that. I meant what you wore today is fine. There's no need to go and get changed. You can have a shower here. And if you want to wear clean clothes, we can put your clothes in the wash right now, spend another two hours in bed, and they'll be dry by the time we're ready for dinner. I wouldn't have suggested dinner if I'd realised you'd want to leave.'

'I don't want to leave. Not really. But I'd love to have dinner in your restaurant and I want to wear something nice. And besides, if we're spending the day together tomorrow, I need to have clean clothes for that.'

He'd been reluctant to let her go, and they'd stopped and kissed every five seconds or so as they walked arm-in-arm to her car.

'At least, this time I'm not chasing after you down my drive,' he'd joked.

She'd cocked her head to one side. 'Why did you chase after me?'

'You know why.' He'd kissed her again. 'Because just like now, I didn't want you to leave.'

'But you know I'll be coming back this time. Or meeting you at the restaurant at 8, I should say.'

'I still think I should come and pick you up.'

She'd grinned. 'What? To make it feel more like a real first date? We've just spent the last six hours in bed. And twenty hours or so before that. I think we're way past first date stuff. Plus me getting a cab means you'll have more time to catch up with things you need to do.'

When he'd asked her to have dinner with him at his restaurant he'd said it was because that was what they had planned to do when he'd asked her for their first date, the day they met. And they hadn't actually been on a real date yet.

'Fine. I do need to make a few calls. This is crazy, but I'm missing you already and you haven't even left yet.'

'Then I'd better go. The sooner I leave, the quicker I'll be back.'

But their 'goodbye for now' kiss had lasted for at least ten minutes, and had become so intense that they almost had sex on the drive, until some squabbling seagulls nearby made them remember where they were.

She was definitely in love with Mikkel and she wanted the world to know it.

Ben and Angela already knew how she felt. Now it was time she told her dad. And also her sister, Bethany.

But first she needed to call the Turners and ask for a little more time to consider their proposal.

Because there was something else she wanted to discuss with her dad and she wasn't sure how he would take it.

But she knew she had to ask.

Twenty-Seven

Mikkel watched Portia drive away and waited until her car was out of sight before going back inside.

He knew he was in love with her and he was fairly certain she felt the same. That made him feel wonderful.

But it was also rather worrying.

Portia's life revolved around luxury hotels and business deals; her dad was on a Rich List. She had travelled extensively and was used to mega-yachts, private planes, and obviously, five-star hotels. Could she be happy in Seahorse Harbour? Mikkel's life was here. Leaving wasn't an option for him.

But neither was losing Portia.

How would this all pan out?

If she got Seahorse Harbour Holiday Park, she'd have a reason to stay. Or at least to come back often. That would give their relationship a chance.

But what if she didn't get the site? What

would happen then? Would she simply say, 'This has been fun,' and then walk away?

There was a possibility he might meet her friends. Surely that must mean she was thinking he'd be in her future?

He couldn't worry about this now. He was seeing her again in a couple of hours. They were spending the night together and all day tomorrow. They had time to discuss the future.

He went back inside and switched his phone from silent. He glanced at the list of missed calls and texts. Apart from one call from his dad and a text to say they'd chat later, all the other nine missed calls and an equal number of texts, were from Diana.

Something must've happened for her to call and text that much. He checked each text in turn but all of them read the same, or something very similar: "Call me back, Mikkel. It's urgent. I really need to speak to you."

He hesitated for just a moment before taking a long, deep breath. Feeling a little anxious, he pressed the icon to call her.

Twenty-Eight

'I tell you I heard him say it, with my own ears.'

Portia felt as if she'd been hit by not just one truck but by several and she gripped the church wall surrounding the tiny cemetery of St Mary Star of the Sea, to prevent herself from collapsing in a broken heap. Because that's how Lilith Shoe's news had made her feel... Broken.

Her cab from Easterhill had got caught behind the final practice run of the Easter Bonnet and Carnival Parade that was meandering along Church Row. Jonno, her cab driver again today informed her that it would have already snaked its way around the village and gone up Seahorse Cliffs towards The Weeping Eye and was now making its final descent towards the church hall.

'I got caught behind it yesterday,' he said. 'They take the same route every year. It ends at the church hall, where tomorrow a large and delicious afternoon tea and an abundance of Easter Eggs will be waiting for every participant and all the spectators.'

'Mikkel told me about it. We're planning to watch the parade together on Easter Sunday afternoon.'

'Are you? That's good news. I hope you'll both be wearing Easter bonnets,' Jonno laughed. 'Sandra's making ours. She loves these things.'

'I'll have to have a word with Mikkel. But I'm sure we'll find something suitable.'

She and Jonno had chatted about Seahorse Harbour and several other topics during this trip from her hotel, but for some reason, on this occasion they hadn't mentioned Mikkel until now.

'We'll see you tomorrow then. I'll be able to introduce you to my lovely wife.'

'I'll look forward to meeting her. Er. Rather than keep the engine ticking over until the road's clear, I may as well walk from here. It's only a couple of minutes' from here down to Sea Walk, I think, and it's such a lovely evening.'

After paying Jonno and giving him a generous tip, she thought she spotted Lyn, from Seahorse Bites Café and she dashed through a gap in the procession to nip across the road and say a quick hello. Except it wasn't Lyn, just someone very like her.

She had to wait for another gap to cross the road again and said, 'Excuse me, please,' to a cluster of women blocking the pavement, their heads so close together and their shoulders hunched, that they looked like a rugby scrum.

'Oh hello dear,' one of them said.

It took a second or two for Portia to recall who the woman was but the small stature, ginger hair, rosy cheeks and freckled face definitely rang a bell. And then she had it. Lilith Shoe, the woman who had been gossiping in Beach Bakers and Seahorse Bites Café.

'Hello. Sorry to barge through but the parade is taking up the road and there's not much room to move.'

'Nothing to be sorry about,' Lilith said. 'This is the practice run for tomorrow's parade. It's much later than it should be. Some of these children should be in bed at this time of night. It should've started at 6 but Tina Burroughs was late, as usual, and then Pumpkin Peacock was sick all over the vicar. Who names their child Pumpkin? That's her Christian name, you know. Nothing Christian about Pumpkin, if you ask me. Some mothers these days.' She tutted again.

'Yes. If you'll excuse me, I mustn't be

late.'

It had taken longer than she expected to get here, even allowing for extra traffic after the experience of earlier that morning and she wished she hadn't crossed the road to say hello to Lyn, especially as it wasn't Lyn. The last thing she needed was to get caught in a conversation with Lilith. The church clock chimed and Portia glanced up to see that it was about to strike the hour.

She'd only be a few minutes late and Mikkel wouldn't mind but she didn't want to waste a second longer than she had to. She was eager to see him again.

Lilith Shoe placed a hand on Portia's arm and squeezed. She had a vice-like grip.

'How are you feeling, dear?' Lilith said, pulling her away to one side so that the rest of the women Lilith had been with had to strain to hear.

And they were. All of them. Portia could see that.

'I'm feeling fine, thank you.' She was surprised by the question. 'In fact, I'm feeling wonderful.'

Lilith gave her a sympathetic smile and nodded.

'Good for you, dear. That's the spirit. Put on a brave face and don't let him see you're hurting. Because you must be, of course. Is that why you ran from his house after spending the night? Did he tell you what they were doing? Did you already know of their plans? It's deceitful, that's what it is. And wrong in so many ways. Alex may not be perfect. In fact, we all know he's far from an angel himself. But the poor man nearly died, and he's promised to change his ways. Now she does this. And with Mikkel. I expected better of him. We all did. But men are men and we women are merely pawns. Not that Diana's a pawn. Oh no. She thinks she's a queen. And I suppose Mikkel thinks he's her knight in shining armour. I'll lay good money on it ending in disaster.'

'I'm sorry. What? I don't understand what you're saying. Are you … are you suggesting something's happened between Mikkel and Diana?'

'Happened? I should say so. Diana's leaving Alex and moving in with Mikkel. They're waiting until after the Easter holidays and her kids have gone back to their schools in London but then they're announcing it to the world. It's shocking. Are you saying you didn't know? Oh dear. How awful. I thought you did.'

'I … I think you must be mistaken.' Portia could hardly say the words. 'It can't possibly be true.'

Lilith tutted and shook her head, her tight ginger curls bobbing about her rosy cheeks like worms on hooks.

'I couldn't believe it myself at first. You wouldn't know this of course, you not being local, and I'm not one to gossip, but Diana and Mikkel have been ... involved for quite some time. Oh yes. They were all friends at first. Her, Alex and Mikkel. Then last Easter she and Mikkel had a fling. That's all it was supposed to be. You know what these men are like. Well, of course you do. You ... but I won't embarrass you about that. Mikkel is handsome and charming and he certainly has a way with women. You fell under his spell just like all the rest, so don't blame yourself, dear. And it's best that you know now, isn't it?'

'You're wrong. This is nonsense.'

'There's no need to take that tone. I'm only saying what I heard.'

'How did you hear it? When?'

'Earlier this evening. They were in The Seahorse Inn car park and I was the other side of the hedge. Just walking up from The General Store, minding my own business. I heard Mikkel's laugh and I saw Diana through a gap in the hedge and ... I admit I got a little closer, but only because I had a feeling they were up to no good. And I was right.'

'No. You misunderstood. Excuse me. I must go.'

The grip tightened.

'I'll tell you what they said, word for word and you can be the judge.'

Portia should've walked away but she couldn't seem to move.

'Mikkel said, "So that's the plan. You'll leave Alex and move in with me and we'll announce it to the world when Becca and Toby have gone back to school." Then Diana said, "Yes. But we can still be together before then. I'm finally sure of what and who I want. You sleeping with Portia, and giving me that ultimatum made me see sense. We'll be together Mikkel and I promise you it'll be for the rest of our lives." I have an excellent memory and I can assure you that is word for word.' Lilith gave a small cough. 'They might've said more if I hadn't stumbled and fallen through the hedge. They saw me and dashed away. Well, Mikkel did offer to help me but as if I'd let him. I liked that man, but not anymore. Those poor children. And poor, dear Alex. Oh my. Is that Lenny Tripp and his new woman? I must go, dear. Take care now.'

Lilith released her grip and scuttled off, along with her group of cronies.

Portia dropped down onto the church wall and tried to catch her breath.

Surely none of that could be true? It couldn't.

But Lilith had said Diana had mentioned

Mikkel giving her some sort of ultimatum.

Had Portia got Mikkel completely wrong? Had he only slept with her to make Diana jealous? Had he been the one telling lies? The one being deceitful. The one who would do anything to get what he wanted.

And clearly, it this were true, it wasn't just Seahorse Harbour Holiday Park he wanted. He also wanted Diana.

Portia may have unwittingly helped him to get both.

Diana was leaving her husband, perhaps in part because she had realised how much Mikkel really meant to her once she'd discovered he had slept with Portia.

And Portia had been ready to give him the holiday park. Well, half the holiday park to be precise.

She'd been prepared to do something she'd never done before. Two things, in fact.

One – she'd fallen in love.

Two – she'd asked her dad to agree to a joint venture with Mikkel Meloy.

'Because I love him, Dad,' she had said when she'd called Tommy just over an hour ago. 'And as crazy as this may sound, I'm pretty certain we're going to be spending the rest of our lives together.'

Which just served to show that she wasn't always right.

And sometimes, like today, she could be

utterly and completely, wrong.

Twenty-Nine

Portia shoved open the door of Hippocampus and stormed over to where Mikkel was chatting to one of his waiters. It was as if he could tell she was there and he turned his head and beamed at her.

'Wow! You're more gorgeous each time I see you. You take my breath away.'

'And you've taken mine. When were you going to tell me? Or weren't you? Were you hoping I'd leave once the deal was done and then you and Diana could set up your cosy home together and you'd have everything you ever wanted?'

'What?' His brows knit together and he stared at her. 'Me and Diana? Oh shit. I should've told you about Diana.' He closed his eyes tight and shook his head.

Portia's mouth fell open. Was that it? Was that all he had to say?

'I'm really sorry, Portia. But it's over.'

He hurried towards her and he looked

genuinely contrite.

'Clearly. But it never really got started, did it? You had the nerve to accuse me of lying when all this time it's been you! Or was that all part of your plan? An act? A way to get me to do what you wanted? I don't get it. I don't understand how I could be so wrong about you.'

'What?' He reached out for her but she slapped his hand away. 'I … I don't understand. What's going on? What are you saying? That you think I've been using you? How? Why? What plan? I haven't lied to you. I didn't tell you about Diana and I realise now that was a mistake. A huge mistake. And I'll admit that, for a moment or two, I didn't know what to do about her. About us. About me and Diana, that is. Not that there was a me and Diana. Not since before Christmas. Sorry. I don't suppose this is making sense. But why are you so angry? No. I can see why you might be. Please let me explain. It's not as bad as you seem to think. At least I don't think it is.'

Portia wasn't sure of anything now. He'd just said he and Diana weren't a couple. Hadn't he? Or was he saying they weren't a couple since before Christmas, but now they were? She was totally bemused.

'Okay. Explain.'

'Shall we sit down?'

He pointed to a cosy corner. A cosy, romantic corner where a table was laid for dinner for two, with a crisp, white linen cloth scattered with petals from a red rose, and a bottle of champagne chilling in an ice bucket beside the table.

She glared at him but walked on shaky legs to the table and sat on the chair he held out for her.

'Okay. I'm listening.'

'Would you like a drink?'

'No. Just an explanation.'

He gave her a half smile, poured himself a glass of water and gulped it down.

'It's a long story and if you want to hear every bit of it, I promise I'll tell you, but for now all you really need to know is that Diana and her husband, Alex were going through a rough patch around this time last year and Diana turned to me for ... comfort. We had a brief affair and I fell for her. I wanted more, which she didn't feel she could give. Last summer she came back for the holidays, which she and the kids always did. Alex didn't come with her and Diana and I spent some time together again. I was still in love with her. At least I thought it was love. Now I'm not so sure it was. Not true love, anyway.' He smiled oddly. 'Now that I know what true love really is. But we'll come back to that in a minute. Josie was here for the summer and

Diana decided it was time for some changes. She left Alex and she and I had a relationship which, at the time, I hoped would last. She changed her mind and went back to Alex. But just this week, she seems to have had doubts and she called me to ask if we could pick up where we left off. I'd just finished talking to her the day you and I met. I'd given her an ultimatum. I told her that nothing could happen between her and me while she was still with Alex. I honestly didn't think she'd leave him. And I hadn't thought it through. And then you came into my life and I knew almost immediately that I could never go back. That I no longer wanted Diana because now all I wanted, all I could think about was you. And it's not a lie, or a plan, or a passing fancy, or anything like that. It's love, Portia. It's True Love.' He grinned suddenly. 'It's True Love, Portia Trulove.'

And for a second, she returned his grin and her heart soared. But she remembered Lilith's words.

'And Diana? Lilith told me she heard you two talking this evening. That you said the plan was that Diana would leave Alex after Easter and move in with you.'

He let out a short sigh and a snort of derision.

'Oh God.' He ran a hand through his hair. 'I did say that. But Lilith only heard me repeating the plan as Diana had just told it to me. It was Diana's plan, not mine. And I was so surprised I repeated it to her to try to make sense of it. Diana said I'd got it right, or something like that. I can't even recall exactly what we said. But I do remember Lilith crashing through the hedge. And frankly, it serves her right. But, if she hadn't she would have then heard what I told Diana after that. That I was sorry but that I didn't want her to leave Alex. Not for me. Because I had finally realised that she and I had no chance of a future together. And when she insisted on knowing why, I told her it was because I was in love with someone else. You. And that you'd made me see that what I'd felt for her was only a fraction of what I feel for you. I told her I was going to ask you to spend the rest of your life with me. Either here, in Seahorse Harbour, or anywhere else you want to be, because all I want, Portia Trulove, is you. I don't even want the holiday park anymore. Just you. Just you and nothing else.'

Portia sat in stunned silence and stared at him.

He was telling the truth, she could see it in his eyes. In the desperate look he was giving her as if he had no idea what she would say but that her words could either make or break him.

And suddenly Diana didn't matter. Nothing mattered. Because all she wanted was him.

Which she already knew.

She burst out laughing and shook her head.

'Is something funny?' He sounded terrified.

'Yes. Very. Because I've realised Mikkel Meloy that I don't want Seahorse Harbour Holiday Park either. At least, not without you. I love you too, Mikkel. In fact, I think I can say I adore you. And I've spoken to my dad and we rather like the sound of a luxury eco hotel. We'd even make an exception and consider a joint venture. If you were to be interested in such a scheme. That way both of our dreams can come true.'

He jumped up and pulled her to her feet, kissing her deeply and for quite some time.

'I can't believe my luck,' he said, when they finally eased apart. 'All I dreamt of was a little eco hotel but now I've got the world in my arms. Because you are my world, Portia. And yes, I'll do anything you want. I'll happily go along with any scheme you have if it means I can spend my life by your side.'

'Any scheme? Any plan? Anything at all?'

He nodded with a blissful smile.

'Anything at all.'

'Excellent! Because what I really want. And to my astonishment have wanted almost from the moment we first met, is to spend my life with you. And what I also want is for us to have a family. I want to have a baby with you, Mikkel. Is that too much too soon?'

His mouth fell open before curving into a smile of pure delight.

'I've been thinking about that too. Ever since that phone call with your friends. Nothing would make me happier. Oh. Except perhaps, one thing.' He got down on one knee and produced a ring. A large diamond that sparkled in the soft lighting in the cosy corner of the restaurant. 'This was my grandmother's engagement ring and she and my grandfather were married for more than seventy years. He proposed to her on the day they met and they were in love until the day he died. Will you marry me, Portia Trulove? Will you be my wife and spend the next seventy years, or however long we've got, with me?'

This was crazy. This was insane. But it was real and it was true and it was everything she had ever dreamed of having.

'Yes, Mikkel. Oh, yes. I've never wanted anything as much as I want to be your wife. And this is one deal that doesn't need any negotiation.'

Coming soon

To find out about my next book, and all future releases, please go to: https://www.emilyharvale.com and subscribe to my newsletter via the 'Sign me up' box. Or follow me on social media. There are lots of exciting and wonderfully romantic stories coming soon.

Stay in touch with

Emily Harvale

If you want to be one of the first to hear Emily's news,
find out about book releases, see covers, and enter free
competitions, then sign up to her Readers' Club by
visiting:

www.emilyharvale.com

and subscribing to her newsletter via the 'Sign me up'
box. If you love Emily's books and want to chat with
her and other fans, ask to join the exclusive

Emily Harvale's Readers' Club
Facebook group

Or come and say 'Hello' on social media:

 @EmilyHarvaleWriter

 @EmilyHarvale

 @EmilyHarvale

A Note from Emily

Thank you for reading this book. If you loved it and want to be the first to find out about my new books, and also, chat with me and other fans, ask to join the exclusive Emily Harvale's Readers' Club Facebook group. Or go to: www.emilyharvale.com and subscribe to my newsletter via the 'Sign me up' box.

A little piece of my heart goes into all my books and when I send them on their way, I really hope they bring a smile to someone's face. If this book made you smile, or gave you a few pleasant hours of relaxation, I'd be delighted if you'd tell your friends.
I'd also love it if you have a minute or two to post a review. Just a few words will do, and a kind review makes such a difference to my day – to any author's day. Huge thanks to those of you who do so, and for your lovely comments and support on social media. Thank you.
A writer's life can be lonely at times. Sharing a virtual cup of coffee or a glass of wine, or exchanging a few friendly words on Facebook, Twitter or Instagram is so much fun.

I mentioned my newsletter just now. It's absolutely free, your email address is safe and won't be shared and I won't bombard you, I promise. You can enter competitions and enjoy some giveaways. In addition to that, there's my author page on Facebook and there's also my lovely, Facebook group. You can chat with me and with other fans and get access to my book news, snippets from my daily life, early extracts from my books and lots more besides. Details are on my website but you'll find all my contact links in the Contact section following this.

I'm working on my next book right now. Let's see where my characters take us this time. Hope to chat with you soon. In the meantime, I'm sending you love and virtual hugs. I can't wait to bring you more stories that I hope will capture your heart, mind and imagination, allowing you to escape into a world of romance in some enticingly beautiful settings.

Acknowledgements

My grateful thanks go to the following:

Christina Harkness for her patience and care in editing this book.
My webmaster, David Cleworth who does so much more than website stuff.
My cover design team, JR.
Luke Brabants. Luke is a talented artist and can be found at: www.lukebrabants.com
My wonderful friends for their friendship and love. You know I love you all.
All the fabulous members of my Readers' Club. You help and support me in so many ways and I am truly grateful for your ongoing friendship. I wouldn't be where I am today without you.
My Twitter and Facebook friends, and fans of my Facebook author page. It's great to chat with you. You help to keep me (relatively) sane!

Printed in Great Britain
by Amazon